TRAITORS
IN THE VORKUTA GULAG

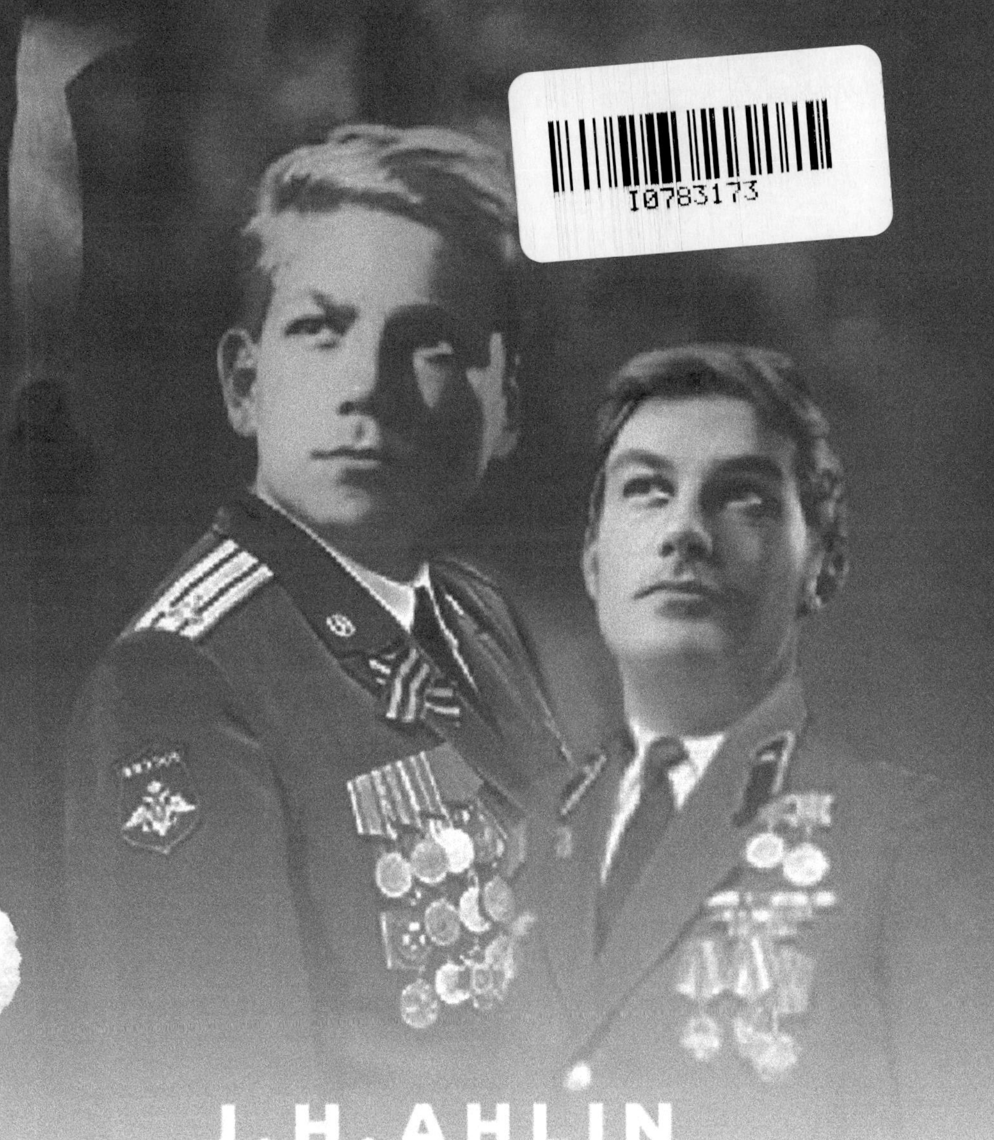

J.H. AHLIN

Kravitz & Sons

INNOVATORS IN PUBLISHING, MARKETING AND ADVERTISING

Kravitz and Sons LLC
204 E Arlington Blvd. Suite B
Greenville, NC 27858

Published by Kravitz and Sons LLC.

ISBN: 979-8-89639-543-0 (sc)
ISBN: 979-8-89639-544-7 (e)
ISBN: 979-8-89639-545-4 (hb)

Dedication

"Traitors in Vorkuta" is dedicated to those American men and women who lost their lives or were injured in conflicts around the world, which were meant to preserve and solidify freedom for people everywhere.

And to the citizens of the Soviet Union who have lived in constant fear of the Gulag system of slave-labor camps and their government from the October Revolution in 1917 – to unfortunately the present day.

Table of Contents

Prologue

⟡

My name is Jenz Ramsgrund. I was born in Düsseldorf, Germany, in September, 1920. I grew up and lived in Nazi Germany until I came to America after World War II and settled in a small-town west of Boston, Massachusetts. My colleague and best friend, Ezekiel Levin, and I had been instrumental in deliberately hindering the development of the V-I and V-II Nazi missile programs during World War II.

I had to flee my beloved Germany because the Gestapo was still quite active, even though hostilities with the Allies and Russians had ended in May, 1945. Ezekiel and I had done considerable damage to the German State Secret Police or Gestapo during the late 1930s and early 1940s. Not only had we eliminated many of their agents, but I had also destroyed their regional headquarters office in Hamburg after one of their "interrogation" sessions.

After that interrogation, I had turned the gas valve on full and left a couple of cigarettes burning on the edge of a chair in a closed and locked room the Gestapo agents had used as a torture chamber for me. The resulting gas explosion destroyed the building and records of my family's Jewish heritage.

Ezekiel's parents were not so fortunate. They were caught in a round-up of Jews right after Kristallnacht on the night of November 9th and 10th in 1938. We could never discover where the Gestapo had taken his parents, although we suspected they might have been brought to Dachau.

Zeke and I discussed our time working for the *Wehrmacht* (German Army) at the Reich's secret rocket research facility on Germany's north coast in Peenemünde in *Traitors in the Gestapo.* The man in charge of the secret rocket base, General Walter Dornberger, gave us orders to find out why his Jewish slave laborers were dying at an alarming rate.

V

Ezekiel and I were ordered to travel to some of the concentration labor camps to find out the reason for the deaths of so many Jewish slave workers. It was a mystery for the general because the general's Jewish workers were given similar housing and rations as his enlisted personnel. Ezekiel and I gave a detailed summary of our findings after visiting the labor camps at Treblinka, Sobibor, and Auschwitz to General Dornberger in *Traitors in Treblinka.*

At the time, Zeke and I thought traveling to the concentration labor camps wouldn't be too dangerous. After all, I was an SS Lieutenant, and Zeke was a Wehrmacht sergeant. We had no idea Treblinka, Sobibor, Balzac, and Auschwitz were not labor camps at all but death camps, *Totenlagers,* whose sole purpose was the destruction and eradication of European Jewry.

General Dornberger ran the secret rocket research facility in Peenemünde on Germany's north coast. He initially didn't put much credence in the report Zeke and I provided for him after we had visited the death camps. He couldn't believe the Reich was killing every Jew entering the camps. He called each of the camp commanders in order to verify our report.

The General was as chagrined as we were. Verifying and certifying the accuracy of our reports, along with other data, led him to believe we might be Jewish. Zeke and I met with the General at an off-site meeting in a local hospital.

His declaration at the meeting: "A person's religion is between him, his family, and God. It should be a private matter, without state interference."

He added that it had been two Jews who had saved his life while imprisoned by the Allies in a French prison camp during the Great War (WW-I).

I eventually found work in America at an engineering company (Raytheon) that was in the process of developing a heat-seeking missile. I had no idea how my knowledge of missile technology was going to prove to be a grave danger to my family.

This is the story of how my good friend Ezekiel and I had to confront evil in a dangerous cat and mouse game with the Stasi police in our native Germany. We were clueless about the pernicious evil exhibited by the Russians in their Gulag * at Vorkuta in Siberia. This prison was one hundred miles north of the Arctic Circle with no roads in or out. The few roads in the village of Vorkuta had to be repaved every year because of the permafrost just beneath the surface.

We were completely baffled at the lengths the Soviets would go to steal technological advancements from United States. Little did Ezekiel and I realize that the pervasive gulag system of fear struck at the heart of every Russian citizen.

The constant atmosphere of fear, betrayal, and the ubiquity of the *NKVD* ** underlined the "generalized cruelty that permeated the culture of the Gulags, and the Soviet Union itself."

It was the later seminal work of Aleksandr Solzhenitsyn as a prisoner in the gulags, chronicler, and author of history, that won him the Nobel Prize in 1970. **His work, *The Gulag Archipelago,* "helped create the world we live in today – a world in which Soviet communism is no longer held up as anybody's political ideal."** ***

---

*Gulag is an acronym, meaning *Glavnoe Upravlenie Lagerei* or Main Camp Administration. The term "Gulag" has become known to most Russian citizens as the repressive Soviet system itself. There were over 400 of these prison camps all over Russia. They were farm gulags, gold-mine gulags, and fish-canning gulags. The gulag at Vorkuta operated a very large coal mine with over 60,000 slave-worker prisoners.

The gulag prison camp system was instituted after the October Revolution in 1917. It lasted until President Gorbachev began the final dissolution of the remaining camps in 1987. Gorbachev's grandfather had been a gulag prisoner. The closest estimates of the numbers of prisoners killed in the *lagpunkts* (prisons) was over 60,000,000 souls between 1917 and 1987. Many of these people were completely innocent; Stalin had people arrested not for what they had done, but for who they were.

**The NKVD was the secret police during the 1930s and 1940s. From the Russian, *Narodnyi komissariat vnutrennikh del,* People's Commissariat of Internal Affairs. The NKVD evolved from the Cheka, *Chrezvychainaya komissiya,* or the secret police during the civil war era. Prime Minister Vladimir Putin, a former KGB agent, proudly identified himself as a Chekist.

***Anne Applebaum, From the Forward of The Gulag Archipelago, Aleksander Solzhenitsyn, New York, NY. Vol 1, Harper & Row, 1976.

Introduction

Zeke, my wife Ilse, and I temporarily moved from the Reich to Sweden and lived with relatives for a few months until the end of hostilities in Germany, in May, 1945. At the end of the war, I discovered that both Ezekiel, my wife Ilsa, and I were on a Gestapo elimination list. Zeke changed his name back to his given name. Vitali Carapezza disappeared. Ezekiel Leven, his original German name, finished his engineering degree at the Technical University in Berlin. He married his sweetheart, Adiya, whom he had rescued from Treblinka and adopted her younger sister, Chasha, whom he had also rescued from Treblinka.

Ezekiel, Adiya, and Adiya's younger sister, Chasha, became instant members of Zeke's family and seemed very happy. Ilse and I moved, really fled, to America.

My grandfather's brother, Hartley, was very instrumental in our move to the state of Massachusetts. His father had worked at the Iver Johnson Arms and Cycle Works as an engineer and machinist in their main factory in Fitchburg, Massachusetts.

Hartley had inherited from his wife an old family farm in the small town of Sudbury, Massachusetts. The farm included a small home and barn; both were in a state of disrepair. The last time anyone had actually lived in the home was in the mid-1920s. There was no running water, but there was a well in the dining room right off the kitchen. There were no toilet facilities, but there was an outhouse off the back of the barn.

Although there was no potable running water, a neighbor, Mr. Albee, supplied us with fresh water. We filled glass bottles with fresh drinking water from his outside spigot from the side of his barn once a week.

There was an attempt at some crude electrical wiring, but it looked a little hazardous with an old 60-amp fuse box and all knob and tube wiring. There was an old rusted gas line coming in from the street for the ancient gas stove. The refrigerator was basically an icebox for keeping food cool.

The icebox was empty except for a half-bottle of fairly decent scotch whisky. Who knows how long the whisky had been there? Hartley once told us his uncle from Norway, Gus, liked to keep his whisky cool so he wouldn't have to water it down with ice!

Ilsa and I were overjoyed. The old family home looked like a palace to us! We moved in with Greta and started to make small improvements as our budget would permit.

I had employment, thanks to one of my school classmates back in Düsseldorf. Marlene had emigrated to America shortly after we were in grade school. She made arrangements for job interviews even before we came to America. I told Ilse that Marlene was my first girlfriend in the first grade. Marlene never made fun of my oversized shape.

Greta enrolled at the local high school near Sudbury Center. She had a little trouble the first year because her English wasn't very decipherable. After her first year, she became quite fluent.

After moving to Sudbury, Ilse and I learned a little about the town's history. Even before the American Revolutionary War, some of my uncles' relatives lived in the Sudbury area and were instrumental in the town's early history in the 1600s. Distant relatives of my great grandparents, the Haynes family, had constructed a garrison home down on Water Row across from the Sudbury River.

The garrison homes were used as safe homes when the Native Americans were active and unfriendly in the area. After the Indians had burned out the Haynes family home on Water Row, in April, 1676, the Haynes family moved up to Concord Road overlooking Grandad's farm. The French and Indian War was gradually forming a base for how the early settlers in the New England area reacted to the Native Americans.

As I am writing about our early experiences in America, I am overcome by waves of abject loneliness. My Ilsa has been gone now for over twenty years, and I still miss her intensely. Greta and my two biological children visit me occasionally, but they have their own families now, and all have busy lives. I really don't expect them to pay much attention to an old geezer like me as I approach my centennial year.

Ezekiel and his family eventually joined me in America and moved to Marlboro, Massachusetts. It was close enough so we could meet regularly and discuss our newfound freedoms. Often, we would share stories of our growing up in Düsseldorf over Sunday dinner at a local restaurant, The Wayside Inn.

In early American Colonial times, The Wayside Inn was just a day's ride from Boston on the highway to New York City. Now the restaurant is a local historic landmark and about halfway between Zeke's family and mine. I should mention that all our wonderful Sunday afternoon dinners were not without incident.

I will try to keep this story and the horror surrounding our trip to one of the largest gulags in Russia without emotion. But, every time I think about Greta and her experience in that cruel and abhorrent prison at Vorkuta, and its' similarity to the concentration camps in my home country, I get terrifying nightmares.

Chapter 1

Gun Violence

This wasn't the first time I had had a firearm thrust in my face. After all, I had survived WW II and suffered plenty of dealings with the Gestapo. However, this was the first time someone had pulled out a Lugar in my own kitchen in my home in America. I had only been in the States a few months and was just getting used to speaking only English and settling in at my new engineering position at Raytheon.

It was late on a chilly, windy, and rainy evening. It was just after 11 O'clock. My wife and daughter, Ilsa and Greta had already gone up to bed for the evening. I was watching some difficult war news about Korea on our small television in the kitchen and had answered a persistent knock on our side door.

It was a dark and somewhat stormy evening. At first, I thought it was just the wind rattling the outer storm door. The light from the kitchen reflected off a well-dressed gentleman whom I thought was asking for directions this late at night.

As I opened the door, the well-appointed fellow pushed his way into my kitchen and pointed a handgun at my head.

The thug holding the gun was pretty tall, about five feet ten inches. He had a pockmarked face with hair greying at the temples and thinning on top. He had a receding chin with a rat-like countenance. He almost resembled a leftover from the Gestapo, but his accent was pure American but tinged with a Russian dialect.

As he pushed his way into our home, he declared:

"Ramsgrund, we told you there would be consequences if you did not produce the specifications for the heat-seeking missile.

"Do you have them here?"

My answer might not have been exactly what this intimidating idiot was looking for, but I had to tell him something. I did not want to see any blanching of his trigger finger as he was waving his firearm in my face.

"Yes, yes." I replied. "The drawings and measurements for the missile are in my briefcase on the kitchen table."

His eyes kept darting around the room with a rapid blinking motion. Perhaps he might have a nervous tick. So, I thought I might try and enhance his comfort and relax him a bit.

He kept talking in a rather loud, almost nervous voice. I noticed a vein popping out and pulsating on his forehead.

My comment was, "Sir, please keep your voice down; my wife and daughter are asleep upstairs; I don't want them disturbed."

He then made an unforgivable and strident comment that really made my blood boil:

"You Jews should all be put to sleep so you wouldn't ever disturb anyone ever again."

That did it for me. His comment brought back too many unpleasant memories of my family being discriminated against and my neighbors being persecuted in my beloved Germany.

I pointed and waved my hand toward the stairway leading up from our kitchen family room in the direction of the second floor.

His rapidly blinking eyes followed my arm motion in the direction of the stairway.

That was all the time I needed.

I grabbed his gun hand and wrenched his arm so the pistol was pointed directly under his chin. I placed my thumb over his trigger finger and slowly squeezed.

As I was squeezing his trigger finger, I advised him, "Never use any anti-Semitic language in my home ever again."

I further advised him. **"If you want to live, quickly give me the name of whoever sent you here!"**

"They will kill me!"

"You will be dead very quickly, if you do not immediately divulge the name of the person who sent you to my home."

He whimpered, "It was Schroder, Schroder the guard! Please don't kill me.

He then pulled on my elbow with his free hand. That was all it took to discharge his weapon.

Bang!

The resulting explosion took the top of his head off and spattered blood and brains all over my ceiling. The very dead intruder dropped like a sack of potatoes. Most of the top of his head bounced off my ceiling and landed on my kitchen floor.

Both Ilsa and Greta came running down the stairs directly into the kitchen. The smell of gunpowder was strong in the air. I was hoping the gunshot hadn't penetrated the floor upstairs.

The disgusting pile of human remains on the kitchen floor made for quite a spectacle. There was blood and parts of his skull everywhere. There were fragments of flesh with hair attached all around the kitchen.

Fortunately, both Ilsa and Greta had seen much worse during the war, so they were not totally shocked. Greta had seen Zeke and me dispatch two Gestapo thugs in her own home in Nordhausen, in central Germany

"Jenz, what happened? Are you okay?" Called Ilsa.

"Yes. I'm sorry you both have to witness this mess.

"This gentleman came into our home and threatened our family and me. He was trying to get information from me about a project at Raytheon.

"Unfortunately, he made the mistake of pointing a loaded gun in my face."

I quickly looked outside to see if there was anyone else in the car sitting in my driveway. The lights were on, and the car was idling.

I went to our front door and came around the car from the rear. It was a late-model black Mercedes. I probably should have thought to take the dead man's Lugar, but I was in a bit of a hurry.

As I approached the car carefully from the rear, I couldn't see anyone inside. I got in, drove the car to the end of our driveway, shut down the lights and engine, and popped open the trunk.

When I came back into the kitchen, Ilsa and Greta were busy cleaning up the blood and bits of brain tissue. Greta was standing on a kitchen chair sponging down the ceiling.

"Dad," Greta asked. "What are we going to do with this man on the floor?"

"Sweetheart, we have to make the room look like this never happened. Let's wrap his head in a towel and completely clean the room. You and Mom can help me load him into the trunk of his automobile. Please be careful not to touch the car or anywhere near the trunk. I will patch and retouch the ceiling in the daylight tomorrow."

"Jenz, we can't just leave him in the trunk!"

"No, you're right, Ilsa.

"I will drive the car and leave it in the back of the employee parking lot of the Wayside Inn. The lower parking lot is out of the way of tourists and is surrounded by trees and landscaping. No one will notice it for a few days.

"Ilsa, if you could follow me, but park a couple of hundred meters before the Inn. I will walk back through the woods to find you. I will make sure to leave no tell-tail fingerprint or marks on the car."

It was a dark night with limited visibility; there was a light rain falling. On the way to the Inn, I kept wishing I could make the car and its contents disappear into a deep river or lake. The closest river to our house was only a small stream at the bottom of our hill. Pantry Brook could barely hide a coffee cup, let alone a large automobile. Although as I got to know the area, that small brook would yield fresh-water trout in the spring.

My home in Düsseldorf was near the Rhine. I remember disposing of a few despicable members of the Gestapo in that river.

Sudbury was a quiet, small country town. I decided to leave the car where it could be found in a few days with a mystery in the trunk.

I searched the car to make sure that nothing in it could link the authorities back to Raytheon or my work on missile development.

I wiped down all the surfaces I had touched; I got soaked hiking back through the woods to Ilsa, who was waiting in our car.

Chapter 2

America, First Impressions

It took my little family, Ilsa, Greta, and me, about three months to get somewhat comfortable in our new surroundings. The biggest difference we noticed right away was the lack of state control over our lives. We came from a tightly controlled environment where the Sipo, Gestapo, and local police closely monitored our lives, to a much more relaxed atmosphere.

When we arrived in America, our small town had three police officers. Each took an eight-hour shift. Often, when called, the recorded message was to call back during business hours or call over to the next town, the Framingham police office, if it was an urgent matter. Once when I went to the police office to inquire about a lost dog that showed up at our home, there was a "gone fishing" sign on the door.

When I wanted a rifle to shoot pesky woodchucks in my garden, the clerk at the local hardware store said there was no need for state paperwork and just asked how much ammunition I needed. In Germany, before the war, this type of request would have resulted in imprisonment or immediate transfer to a local concentration or labor camp for a period of twenty years.

In reality, imprisonment in a concentration camp was a life sentence. Even very healthy people rarely survived six months on the minimal food and harsh labor, and horrific living conditions that existed in the camps.

As the concentration camps were liberated by the Russians, English, Canadians, and Americans, the whole world could see the results Nazi tyranny had brought to Germany, Poland, and the conquered territories. Virtually all of the camp inmates were completely innocent victims of Nazi rule. Zeke and I could never get those prisons of inhuman horror out of our everyday thoughts and nightly dreams.

The peace and tranquility of our small town seemed almost unreal to Ilsa, Greta, and me. Farms surrounded us. Behind our old farmhouse was a pasture for the neighbor's cows. Beside our house was a small lane that led down to the railroad tracks about a mile away.

At the bottom of our hill was a sharp curve where many a speeding car would have trouble navigating at night. Very few cars came down our street, and even fewer at night. Sudbury was a very quiet town in 1950.

One of the most historic and fun places Ilsa and I discovered when we first moved to this small quiet town was the grounds around the Wayside Inn. The restaurant inside the main building served traditional American meals.

The peaceful surroundings included a building called the Old Grist Mill, a barn with several old carriages, beautiful, well-kept gardens, and the Martha-Mary Chapel. The chapel was named after the first American president's family, George Washington's mother and sister. There were acres of fields, manicured lawns, and old-growth forests surrounding the Inn. One could sense an inner peace just walking around the grounds.

Ezekiel, his wife, Adiya, and Adiya's sister, Chasha, would meet Ilsa, Greta, and me for Sunday dinner on many Sunday afternoons before Isla and I had our own children. The Wayside Inn provided a quiet atmosphere for our rather cloistered dinners. We would often meet in a quiet corner of the main dining room or in another smaller dining area referred to as the Old Kitchen. We felt comfortable speaking quietly in our native German, if we were away from other diners.

The main dining room had pale blue walls and could seat at least 100 people. The white tablecloths and napkins gave the room an aura of formality and elegance. It was absolutely opulent compared to what we left after the near-total destruction of our hometown of Düsseldorf.

The Inn had historic relevance to the local Americans. It was first noticed in the literature as an operating tavern named Howe's Tavern as early as 1716. There is a marker on the grounds commemorating the passing of General George Washington on his way to New York in 1775.

The dining room serves typical American food, but the menu was always changing slightly. Although on the bland side, most of the food was delicious. Our families always tried to sit in a more secluded area of the dining room or Old Kitchen so our accents wouldn't get noticed. We would only use our native language if there were no families sitting close to our table.

The paneling on the wall framed wonderful old Currier and Ives prints and paintings of American history. The prints could have been reproductions, but they looked like they might have been on the wall since the Inn was built.

On this particular Sunday, there was a light crowd in the restaurant section of the Inn. The waitress was someone I had never seen before in our previous visits for a late afternoon dinner. Her slight accent portrayed her as European, but she did everything she could to cover up her speech and any accent. She carefully pronounced her words by speaking slowly.

I placed her as Bavarian, but she avoided discussing her background, and we placed our order. As Zeke and I were talking, I noticed the waitress hanging around her station near our table. It looked as if she was trying to listen to our conversation. I casually mentioned this to Ezekiel in a low voice, and he stated back in a quiet voice that he was thinking the same thing.

The waitress seemed like a pleasant enough person with a little bit of excess baggage around the midsection but not terribly overweight. Her hair was pulled back in a rather severe blondish bun, very typical of the Bavarian hairstyle. I'm not sure why I felt this way, but her waitress uniform almost looked like it had a European cut to it.

The six of us had a delightful meal of chicken and ground beef. We tried to concentrate our conversation on the good times we had in our native country. Occasionally our conversation drifted to German engineering and technology. Here we had to be careful about avoiding talk of the war, the suffering of the German people, or how fortunate we were to be able to be in America.

Our waitress asked if we would like any of the wonderful desserts offered by the Inn, but we politely declined. Our plates were cleared, and our water glasses were refilled.

I noticed an envelope where my plate had been. I motioned to Zeke and asked if he had seen anyone or the waitress place it there.

"Ezekiel, did you or Adiya notice if the waitress placed this envelope under my plate while serving or clearing our dishes?"

"What is it, Jenz? Was it under your plate during dinner?"

My terse comment was, "Let's ask the waitress when she comes for the bill. It looks like a plain white business envelope."

Adiya asked, "Is there a note or bill inside?"

Out of curiosity, I opened the unsealed envelope; a note fell out:

We know you work at Raytheon in their Avionics department. If you provide the information we want about the heat-seeking missile, your family will not be harmed. The 4th R.

Chapter 3

The Disappearing Waitress

I passed the note around to Adiya, Ilsa, Chasha, and Ezekiel. There was a look of concern on everyone's face.

Zeke asked, "Who could have sent such a note?"

Ilsa spoke up with some authority. "We should ask the waitress; she must have slipped it under your plate as she was clearing the dishes.

My comment was, "Zeke, have you heard anything about the Fourth Reich?"

"I heard somewhere there was another Nazi who popped up on the radar a while back after being released from prison. I think his name was Remer.[*]

Adiya asked, "Is this general dangerous?"

"Any of these Nazis can be dangerous," was Zeke's comment. "I would like to know how they tracked us to this small town in Massachusetts.

"I'm not sure if the 4th Reich is a bunch of hothead old Nazis or a bunch of Nazi want-a-bees. Either way, Zeke, I agree, they could be dangerous. I may ask Marlene, the woman who helped with my finding employment if I should go to my employer or the police with this note."

---

[*]General Otto Ernst Remer was involved in stopping the coup against Hitler by arresting Claus Von Stauffenberg after an attempt on Hitler's life. Remer was arrested by the Allies during the Battle of the Bulge and sent to prison. On his release from prison in 1950, Remer involved himself in Neo-Nazi politics by forming the Socialist Reich Party, which was banned in 1952. Remer fled to Egypt and was involved in the arms trade with the PLO. He died in Spain in 1987 of natural causes.

Ilsa spoke up. "Jenz, we should avoid the local police. There might be too many questions about our activities in Germany during the war."

I went to the front desk and asked for the manager. Mr. Frank Kopias wasn't at the front desk, but the clerk called him from his upstairs office, and he came right down. I wanted to ask about the waitress who had served us our dinner.

"Sir. I would like to pay our check. The waitress who served us didn't come back to collect it. Perhaps you could tell me her name?

"She was the blond woman with her hair drawn up in a bun on the back of her head. She had a slight accent, perhaps Bavarian, and a bit overweight."

"That sounds like Gertie. She hasn't worked here for months, so you must mean someone else. We have no one on our wait staff today that even resembles the waitress you are describing."

"Okay," was my reply. "What do we owe for this bill?"

We all walked outside where we could talk without being overheard. There was a chill in the fall air with a darkening blue sky, suggesting a shortening of the days as we marched toward the winter solstice.

"Ezekiel," I asked. "What do you think about our disappearing waitress?"

"I haven't a clue. But I would be careful about how we approach someone about a threatening note. Perhaps you could ask around at your office who might lend a sympathetic ear without going directly to the local police."

Dark thoughts kept swirling around in my head: how did the waitress get into the restaurant to deliver the note from the 4th Reich? Her contact obviously knew who we were. How was she able to disappear smoothly after making sure I read her note? Was her contact someone from my office? I had to be very discreet when talking with anyone at Raytheon.

It was such a beautiful fall day with just a few puffy clouds on the horizon. I wasn't about to let this intrusion ruin my time with Ilsa and my friends.

The next day I confided with my immediate boss at the plant, Mr. Jerry Lobell.

"Jerry, who can I talk with about a serious personal yet delicate problem?"

"Most of these issues are referred to our health department," explained Jerry. "We have a physician on staff who is excellent and talks to a number of our workers every week. Dr. Paulus is very prudent and tactful and an excellent physician.

"You can go to his office on the first floor and talk with his receptionist about an appointment, or you can call his office at extension 620. You can usually get an appointment within a few days."

Our plant was a rabbit warren of connecting walkways, halls, stairways, and interconnected buildings. The department where I worked, Avionics, took up two floors of an entire building. Doctor Paulus was in an adjacent building connected to our building with a covered walkway. Since I had only been at this facility for a few months, it took me a while to find the doctor's office.

His receptionist was very cordial.

"Mr. Ramsgrund, if you don't mind waiting a few minutes, Dr. Paulus could see you this afternoon. His next patient has canceled his appointment, and I am sure the doctor wouldn't mind seeing you. Could you please fill out this brief personal and health history? The doctor shouldn't be longer than a few minutes."

Chapter 4

⚬⚬⚬⚬⚬

A Disturbing Visit with Our Company's Physician

The wait wasn't long. I was ushered into the doctor's office with the customary pleasantries and asked how long I had been working at Raytheon.

"Good afternoon, Doctor Paulus, thanks for seeing me on short notice."

"It's a pleasure, Mr. Ramsgrund. What can I do for you this afternoon?"

"It isn't a medical problem, doctor. I just wasn't sure where to turn. It concerns my relationship with Raytheon and perhaps some illegal activity."

"I'm not sure I am the correct person to talk with, but please continue."

"I will give you a brief history before I show you the letter I received while having lunch yesterday with my family and friends at the Wayside Inn.

"As you may know from my application and hiring protocol here at Raytheon, I am a recent transplant from my beloved homeland, Germany.

"I worked during the war years as an engineer and member of Hitler's SS. However, my colleague and I secretly did everything we could to slow down the development and production of the V-1 pulse-jet missile and the V-2 rocket. My good friend and colleague, Dr.

Ezekiel Levin, and I were both Jews working in secret to undermine the range, effectiveness, and accuracy of both weapons.

"I believe my familiarity and experience with these weapons might have been helpful for me finding work in the avionics department here at Raytheon."

"You could well be correct, Ramsgrund, but what brings you here today? You mentioned a letter."

"Yes, doctor. It was more of a note."

I handed over the note saying, "I hope you can keep the contents confidential, doctor, until you can tell me the next step and in which direction I should proceed."

The doctor then read the note and raised his eyebrows with a rather perplexed look on his face.

"Ramsgrund, this note is concerning because it hints at and threatens you to transmit priority secret and classified material to possibly third party or foreign government."

"I am well-aware of the implications of the note, doctor. Believe me; the Nazis are dangerous and not to be trusted."

I kept going over possibilities in my mind. Who would know that I worked in a sensitive area of avionics at this company and had knowledge of my life in the Reich?

"Ramsgrund, the doctor interrupted my thoughts; what this note implies is serious. You must bring it to the head of security at this company. I wouldn't wait for a few days or even a few hours."

"What are you suggesting, doctor?"

"I would recommend, Ramsgrund, you let me call directly to Mr. Hammond's office, the head of Raytheon security, and explain this situation to him. I think he will let you know the next step for you to take regarding this threatening note."

"Thanks, doctor, for your time. Should I wait while you call and explain the situation?"

"Yes. But in the meantime, make sure your doors at home are secured at night and be vigilant for strangers around your home. It might help if you had a dog that barks at strange noises or strangers in your neighborhood."

"Thank you, doctor, for your time and suggestions. I will go directly to the security office as soon as they can see me."

"Please take my suggestions for your family's security seriously. This sounds like a dangerous group that has contacted you."

Chapter 5

Central Security Office for the Raytheon Company

The Raytheon security office was located on the ground floor of building A. This building was a bit of a walk from my building C, where the Avionics Department was located, but directly next to and attached to building B.

All the buildings were adjacent to each other but separated by covered walkways. It was explained to me when I joined the Avionics Department that the different buildings aided security and fire control protection for the entire company.

As I approached the office, the only delineation of notice was a small, lettered sign on the upper portion of the entry door labeled "Raytheon Security."

I knocked and went in.

There was a blondish, rather heavy-set woman at the counter behind a bunker-like thick glass enclosure. The glass looked thick enough to be bulletproof, but my thinking at the time was that it seemed hardly necessary.

The blondish woman was very pleasant and asked if I were Mr. Ramsgrund. I guess Dr. Paulus had effectively conveyed news of the note and accompanying threat to my family.

"Yes. I am Jenz Ramsgrund. I am here to see Mr. Hammond."

"Of course! Come this way, sir; he is waiting for you in his office."

She came out from her "bunker" and led me down a long corridor with several offices leading off at right and left angles. Most of the doors were closed, but the one door that was opened looked like a conference room with several cushy chairs around a well-polished mahogany table. There were what looked like sound-deadening panels on the walls and no windows.

The receptionist knocked and entered the next office. The sign on the door stated in bold letters, **Mr. Hammond**.

The assistant for Mr. Hammond was a tall, slender woman who couldn't have been over thirty-five. She had an engaging smile and was dressed very professionally. Since I was happily married to the woman of my dreams, I tried desperately not to think about how she would look without her clothes.

She opened the door that led directly to the conference room we had just passed. She went in before me, closed the door to the hall and threw a switch on the wall, and engaged another button on the mahogany table.

The assistant introduced herself as Stella, then showed me where to sit and explained her actions.

"Sir, the first switch engaged a noise canceling device in the ceiling, and the second button told Mr. Hammond you were here and activated a recording device."

I asked, "Ms. is this always standard procedure?"

"Sir, since you are a Raytheon employee, we need to fully explain these procedures for your benefit. All recordings are analyzed for accuracy and truthfulness. This protects you as well as the company."

Just as the assistant finished her explanation of the procedures, a large man, who was almost my height, walked in and introduced himself.

"Hello, I am Mr. Hammond, head of security here at Raytheon. Dr. Paulus filled me in a bit about your predicament. Could I see the note you received?"

I stood, and we shook hands. "Thanks for seeing me on short notice today, Mr. Hammond. I received this note yesterday while enjoying a late afternoon dinner with my family and friends at the Wayside Inn."

I handed him the note from the inside breast pocket of my sport jacket.

As you can see, it is rather brief and somewhat threatening.

"Thanks for bringing this to my attention, Mr. Ramsgrund. I have read over your file. I'm glad you have not tried to handle this yourself. I am familiar with the way you dealt with some of the members of the Gestapo. Those procedures might not be effective with these folks."

I was starting to squirm a bit in my comfortable chair. How much of my time fighting the Gestapo did these folks know about? Were they aware Zeke and I had eliminated dozens of these Nazi swine?

"Thank you, Mr. Hammond. This note looked like it might involve Raytheon or national security. I wanted to make sure none of the propriety avionics information I was developing got into the hands of our country's adversaries."

"Are you aware, Ramsgrund, of anyone that would consider bringing harm to your family or anyone in particular who would benefit from the information you could transfer to these individuals?"

"I'm not even sure how they tracked me to this area of the country or to this company! The only folks who might have a grudge against me could be members of the Gestapo who discovered the identity of whoever was eliminating their brother officers.

"My family consists of my wife, Ilsa, and stepdaughter, Greta, who is in the local high school. None of us have been in the country long enough to have enemies or even disputes with anybody. Greta is having a little trouble getting used to speaking English all the time, but no, I cannot think of anyone who would want to do us harm.

"What would you suggest as the next step for me to take to counter-act this threat?"

"For the time being, Ramsgrund, I am going to suggest, no insist, that you do nothing. Tomorrow at 10:00 a.m., I will arrange for a meeting of your department head and the vice president of operations at this facility. I would like you to be at this meeting. Would you mind if I kept this note?"

"Of course not, Mr. Hammond. Use it for whatever is best for the company."

"Please, Ramsgrund, keep yourself and your family secure until we know exactly whom we are dealing with here. Let me know immediately if anyone associated with this group tries in the future to contact you in any way."

"Certainly. I will see you here tomorrow morning."

"And please, Mr. Ramsgrund, always be aware of your surroundings and who is near you or your family."

Chapter Six

A Surprising Meeting at Raytheon

I arrived at my office a little early the next morning. I wasn't sure what to expect from my department head or the Vice-President of Operations. There was a note on my desk: *Mr. Ramsgrund, please report to the security office as soon as you arrive today.*

Since I had arrived just after 7:30, I was sure no one would be at the mid-morning 10 a.m. meeting this early.

To my surprise, as I entered the security office, the receptionist ushered me directly into the conference room. The conference table was crowded with several serious-looking gentlemen. It looked somewhat disconcerting to be in a room with a bunch of well-dressed gentlemen I didn't know.

Mr. Hammond began with introductions.

"Jenz, please come in and have a seat here at the far side of the conference table."

It was a little intimidating to be seated with all these distinguished-looking gentlemen. It was curious that they were all here this early.

I recognized our department head of Avionics, but there were three others I couldn't place. One of them was probably the VP of Operations, but who were the other two men?

"Gentlemen." Mr. Hammond began.

"Gentlemen. I think we have to take this note and threat seriously. The FBI considers this a national security threat and a direct threat to the Ramsgrund family, who received this note.

"This is Mr. Jenz Ramsgrund. He came to us here at Raytheon directly from the secret rocket base in Peenemünde, Germany, where, as a covert member of the Nazi SS, he was intimately aware of the guidance and propulsion engineering systems for the V-1 pulse-jet missile and the V-2 rocket. His close knowledge of the Gestapo, and his accomplishments of eliminating dozens of its member agents, have perhaps followed him to our company.

"Jenz, to your right is Dr. Clemson, your department head of Avionics." He stood, gave a rather quick smile, which looked more like a grimace, and shook my hand.

"Next is our Vice President of Operations, and a member of our board of directors, Mr. Vince Oberton." He stood and waved hello. His smile seemed a little more genuine than my department head's.

"Following around the table, Captain Seth Dobrinsky, from the Naval War College in Newport, Rode Island." He stood and extended his arm with a slight wave of his hand. It was a little disconcerting to me that it almost resembled a Hitler salute. He didn't smile.

"And finally, Jenz, this is Mr. Colyard Johnsen from the Boston office of the Federal Bureau of Investigation."

He didn't stand, wave, or smile. He just nodded. He did say 'good morning' almost as an afterthought.

My immediate thought was, jeez, I've really stepped in it now. If Zeke were here, I'm sure he could help me through my abject nervousness. He would be able to explain our relationship with past Gestapo creeps better than I. My palms started to get sweaty; I could feel the moisture starting to stick my back to my undershirt. Everyone in the room was staring at me. War College, FBI, what the devil is going on here?

"First, let me assure you, Jenz, information about this threatening note will not leave this office unless marked 'Secret/Classified.'

"Second, your neighbor has allowed us to park an unmarked, older automobile in his side yard. This will be used for 24-hour surveillance of your front and side doors. The windows of the automobile have been treated with a very dark tint. No one will be able to see inside. The home is now occupied by a cooperating family but used to be a roadside tavern in the 1930s.

"Third, your phone will be tapped, so any telephone threats to you or your family will be monitored."

"This sounds like very comprehensive protection for my family. Are you sure this one threat requires such security?"

Mr. Hammond replied.

"You will understand our concerns, Jenz, once you perceive how we will handle the implications not expressed by the author of this note.

"Let me understand your family dynamics. You have a wife, Ilse, and a stepdaughter, Greta. And Greta is a third-year high school student at the local high school in Sudbury Center."

"Yes, that is correct."

"Your friend, Ezekiel, and his family from Germany were at dinner with your family when you received the note?"

"Yes," I replied.

"His family consists of his wife, Adiya, and his wife's sister, Chasha, who is sixteen and a second-year student at the same high school in Sudbury Center."

"Correct. Both girls are at the same school even though the Leven family lives in Marlboro. The young girls had no friends when they first came to America. Both girls had been severely traumatized by what they witnessed in Nazi Germany during the war.

"Adiya was approximately five minutes from entering the gas chamber at Treblinka when Ezekiel and I saved her and her younger sister, Chasha."

Captain Dubinsky from the Naval War College waved his hand and asked a question. "Just how did you accomplish their safety, Mr. Ramsgrund?"

"Sargent Leven and I were sent to Treblinka under orders from our commanding officer, General Walter Dornberger. He ordered us to check on the health and well-being of the Jewish prisoners at this camp.

"The general wanted to understand the reason for the sickness and death from exhaustion of his workers residing at the secret rocket base at Peenemünde in northern Germany.

"We were also ordered to send back to the rocket base a number of healthy men or women who would aid our efforts in building, testing, and perfecting the V-l and V-ll missiles.

"Adiya, now Sargent Leven's wife, had been whipped by a Ukrainian guard because she had asked the Sargent a question. She still has long red scars on her back.

"Sargent Leven helped Adiya off the floor, and she and her younger sister, Chasha, were among the half dozen people we were able to save from the gas chamber. They were sent directly to Peenemünde.

"My stepdaughter, Greta, was quite young when the Gestapo attempted to brutalize and rape her. She eventually had to disguise herself as a male and act as my aide in order to escape the Reich through Denmark and Sweden."

"Good Lord, Ramsgrund. It seems you and your family have quite some hair-raising stories to tell from your experiences with the Gestapo."

"Captain Dubinsky, you have no idea how brutal and effective this group of secret state police were in killing off our Jewish neighbors, friends, and ordinary Germans who protested against the Hitler regime."

The captain had another question. "Has the trauma these young women experienced affected their lives in any way that would make them hard to surveil and protect?"

I had to think hard about that question because of an incident I had witnessed soon after the girls had started high school.

"Both girls have a certain remoteness from their classmates," I answered. "But I think it probably stems from their language difficulties and not knowing any of their peers.

"Both Greta and Chasha are a little intimidated by the boys and male teachers with whom they contact every day at the school. I feel this is understandable considering their history."

Mr. Hammond concluded the meeting mysteriously.

"Thank you all for coming; we will meet tomorrow morning, same time, same place, and implement Operation Lightning Bolt, or OLB, the name the FBI has assigned to this threat."

Chapter 7

Testing My Patience as a Parent

This incident, which I did not bring up at the meeting with the security personnel at Raytheon, tested my will and probably my suitability as a parent.

Both Ilse and I hoped to have a family of our own after we came to America. In a way, we already had a daughter. Greta seemed to blend with our family, even though she was troubled and terrified that she would not be able to see her real father again after we left Sweden for America.

Having a teen-aged daughter with beautiful long blond hair, a full wonderful figure, and an engaging personality was just the start of our struggles as parents. Since Greta didn't grow up with us, Ilse and I were woefully unprepared to deal with teenage girl issues in a new country.

I first met Greta when Zeke and I had lunch in their small family restaurant in their home in Nordhausen, central Germany. Greta was a waitress for her father, the owner. After our meal, Greta begged us to take her with us because of the Russian Army breakthrough at Stalingrad and Kursk.

The following year, when Zeke and I stopped in to see Greta and her dad, they had closed the restaurant, but the Gestapo followed us to her home and attacked Greta and her father. Although Zeke and I prevented Greta from being brutally raped and her father killed, we were completely surprised when her father dropped her off at our secret rocket base and begged us to protect her from the Russians as their army swept across the Reich.

When Greta started at Sudbury High School, she was naturally shy because her only friend was Adiya's younger sister, Chasha. In addition, her English was far from fluent. On top of that, her strong German accent just seemed to remind all the teachers and adults at the school of the Nazi regime and all of the failures of the 3rd Reich.

Ezekiel's adopted daughter, Chasha, had her mother's natural beauty. She had a slim figure, and long shiny brown hair framed her absolutely beautiful facial features. She had a quiet politeness and poise, usually not often seen in teenage girls. None of her new acquaintances at Sudbury High School ever knew she had been minutes away from being gassed by one of the cruelest regimes on the planet at Treblinka.

The high school boys, on the other hand, considered their accent as exotic and their aloofness as being stuck up or too good for them.

In fact, both girls were terrified of all of the boys and young male teachers in the high school. Both young women had seen firsthand the pain and suffering young Nazis males were capable of inflicting.

As the girls struggled through their first year at the high school, they seemed to grow closer to each other and isolate themselves from the other students in their classes. This standoffishness was worrisome for my wife, Ilse; I sloughed it off as being new to the school and new to America.

Often the girls would stay at each other's homes when studying for a test or working on a school project. It was late one fall afternoon when I went up to Greta's room to see if Chasha would like to stay with our family for dinner. There was the smell of burning leaves from our neighbor's yard in the air.

As I was walking down the hall toward Greta's room, I could hear giggling from the room, so I expected them both to be in there. I never thought about knocking, announcing myself, or pausing for even an instant. I just walked right in.

My first glance into the room left me absolutely stunned. Both girls were on Greta's bed without a stich of clothing on! They were hugging each other. My first reaction was a flash of surprise and anger.

I started to yell. **"I will never..."** but then I stopped. My abrupt presents and pause in my sentence startled both girls. They looked at me in shocked panic and horror.

I stopped my angry tirade because I remembered what both of these young women had been through at the hands of the Nazis. Each had escaped humiliation, degradation, abuse, rape, and death from a brutal regime.

Then I quietly finished my sentence.

"I will never, ever, ever, come into your room again or interrupt your privacy while you are doing your homework without knocking and announcing myself."

I said all this while looking out the window.

"I just need to know if Chasha will be able to stay for supper." I kept looking out the window.

"She would like to stay overnight if that is okay with you, Dad."

"Of course, it is okay with Ilsa and me, but check with your folks, Chasha. Dinner is in 30 minutes."

As I backed out of Greta's bedroom without even glancing at either of them. I wasn't sure who was more surprised or embarrassed. I hoped I hadn't irreparably injured the psyche of either young woman. I decided to keep my thoughts and this particular incident to myself.

After I gave the blessing and all through dinner, both girls kept giving me sideways glances. They were probably hoping I wasn't going to bring up their earlier tryst at dinner.

I kept the conversation light and asked questions about school and any projects they might be doing, and after-school activities.

I kept thinking that what I observed was private and should be kept very private.

In order to let them know, it was going to remain private, I related the story General Dornberger had related to us when he discovered Ezekeil and I were Jewish:

General Dornberger told Ezekiel and I that a person's religion was between their family and God and had nothing to do with interference from the Reich or the Wehrmacht.

I told my family while glancing at Chasha and Greta that this was the way I felt about their religion and their private lives. "No matter what you young women decide to do with your lives, from having trusted relationships, choices of boyfriends, or careers.

"As parents we can guide you or answer any questions you might have as you go through school. But, know that we will always love and respect your decisions as you mature. I know you will both be caring and considerate adults, as well as beautiful and gracious young women."

Chapter 8

A Worrisome Development

It was a cool, windy, typical fall morning when I awoke early the next day. The sun wasn't up, but a grey dawn was close. As I rubbed my eyes and looked out the front window, it looked like a car was pulling away from the front of my home. I didn't pay too much attention to it, except it looked like a fairly new late-model black Mercedes.

I showered and ate a quick breakfast of cranberry juice and toast with jam without waking Ilsa or Greta. I never developed a taste for coffee; there was precious little of it in Germany or anywhere in the Reich during the war. What little coffee was to be had tasted like roasted tree bark.

It was almost cold outside; it looked like we had experienced below-freezing temperatures in the nighttime. There was a patina of white hoarfrost on the grass and shrubs.

I had dressed in a white button-down shirt with a sweater vest, sports jacket, and tie. I wanted to look presentable to whoever was at the morning meeting regarding the note I had found under my plate at the Wayside Inn.

As I was leaving by my side door, which exits directly to my driveway, I observed something stuck to the outside of my storm door. After closing the door behind me, I tore off an envelope taped to the glass part of the door. Inside was a brief note:

You were told not to go to the authorities. Your family will now suffer the consequences. If you deliver the information required, your family could be spared.

I immediately stuffed the note and envelope into my pocket and drove to our plant. There was little traffic on the road; I'm sure I exceeded the speed limit most of the way. I did not want my family to worry about this new threat, but it occurred to me that there must be someone at Raytheon who was able to know exactly what was going on at the security meeting. Or, it could be just another intimidating threat to get information on the avionics project I was working on at the plant.

I arrived at my desk just after seven. The sun was just peeking out of low clouds on the horizon. I noticed the security officer as I was on my way to my desk. There was an envelope with my name on it on top of some paperwork. There was a note inside:

Jens Ramsgrund, we know where you live. If you bring home the specks and blueprints to the heat-seeking missile you are helping to develop, we will leave your family alone. Leave the entire package between your side doors this evening—the 4ᵗʰ R.*

How could someone enter these secure offices and leave an envelope on my desk? I immediately approached the security officer, who was just outside the office.

"Has anyone unauthorized been in these spaces overnight?"

The guard seemed friendly enough but replied in a slightly officious tone.

"Of course not! Only the cleaning crew is allowed in these offices during non-working hours."

Somehow, the security guard's comment wasn't very reassuring. The forcefulness of his reply made me think he might be hiding something. Or, perhaps, he was grumpy after staying up all night watching over our workspaces. His facial expression of surprise didn't match his effort at truthfulness. His eyes drifted down and away. He wouldn't keep eye contact with me.

---

*The Sidewinder missile being engineered by Raytheon and the Lockheed Company was developed from a German heat-seeking bomb finished near the end of WW II. William B. McLean initiated U.S. research on this missile at what is now the Naval Air Weapons Center, China Lake, California. The name of the missile comes from the common name (Sidewinder) of a type of rattlesnake that utilizes infrared heat to hunt its prey.

Another emotion troubled me at the time. For the first time since leaving the Reich, I felt an undercurrent of fear. I wasn't sure if it was the guard's voice and facial expressions not matching his words or the unusual quiet of the office. I knew it was early, but usually, there was a low-level hum of early-shift folks coming and going.

A feeling of abject loneliness washed over me. I knew it was irrational, but here I was, standing in the middle of my office cubical with photos of my loved ones framed and decorating the walls surrounding me. Yet, there was something not quite right that I couldn't put my finger on or understand.

I thought about my situation, trembling slightly at the prospect of the unknown, then I understood. Control. I was a big strong man with forces coming against my family, which I couldn't control. At that moment, I decided to take control and punish those who would consider harming my family.

The guard had walked into the adjacent office. I decided to follow him and gently confront him once again with politeness, but perhaps with a little firmer tone.

As I hurriedly walked into the next office, I noticed no one was there. The back door, which leads to a secure lobby, exit, and parking lot, was just closing.

I jogged through the office, flung open the side door, and was confronted with a security guard sitting at his desk.

"Sir," I called out. "Has anyone just come through here?"

"Just the floor guard. I guess his shift was over. He seemed to be in a hurry and went out to the lot for his car."

"Did you happen to see which way he went?"

"I think he went down to the right," the guard responded. "He probably parks in the "C" lot.

I jogged down to the lot, but a car was passing quickly by on the way out of the gate. The security guard was driving.

I jotted down the license plate number to pass on to Mr. Hammond in the Raytheon security office. I needed to make sure the security guard actually worked at the plant.

Perhaps my mind was playing tricks with me. It was just that these mystery notes were making me nervous about my family's safety.

It had been a few days before I was requested at another meeting with the security officials at Raytheon.

After dealing with the intruder in my home from the night before, I was anxious to discuss with the security team any suggestions they might have for me.

Chapter 9

Reaction to the Intruder

After returning to my office, I glanced at my morning's agenda and headed to the security office. I wanted to get Mr. Hammond's opinion of the recent notes I had received. If a foreign government was trying to steal classified material from our plant, no one was going to be too happy about it.

Doctor Clemson, our head of avionics, was the only person in the conference room when I arrived. Dr. Clemson had a Ph.D. in mechanical engineering and had a career in the U.S. Army Air Force before joining Raytheon.

As I entered the room, Dr. Clemson stood, smiled with a bit of a grimace, and greeted me.

"Good morning, Ramsgrund. Have you had any further communication from our unknown source?"

I wasn't entirely comfortable sharing any new information with anyone at the plant. Someone here was aware of the first note I had received at the Wayside Inn. And someone must have leaked my last meeting with the folks in this room.

"I'm not sure if I should wait until…"

Just then, Mr. Hammond entered the room with a cheery "Good morning!" I wasn't too sure how long he would stay in a good mood after I shared my recent information with him.

I repeated a good morning to him and shook his offered hand.

He also had a question.

"Mr. Ramsgrund, have you had any further communications with our unknown letter writer?"

"I can answer you completely, Mr. Hammond, but I must be assured that whatever is discussed here in this room will go no further."

"I can assure you, Jenz, all the security measures and electronic interruption are always in place whenever we discuss confidential material in this conference room."

"Were all electronic measures in place at our first meeting in this room?" I asked.

"Of course, Ramsgrund. Our company and our security organization treat all confidential information very seriously."

"Well, then," I started. "It might be best if these security measures were reviewed and scrutinized a little more carefully."

After my comment, Mr. Hammond got a bit testy.

"What are you talking about, Ramsgrund?"

I then proceeded to stand and spread out the two notes I had received since the first communication.

Mr. Hammond and Dr. Clemson took their time reading and re-reading both notes.

The head of security was the first to speak.

My God, Dr. Clemson. How can a security leak like this get out of this office?

"We should double-check all of the attendees from the first meeting. In addition, who has access to the transcription of the voice track of the meetings in this conference room?"

"Only my trusted and long-time loyal assistant, Stella, can access the voice recordings. She has been with the company for over eight years."

Although I didn't want to interrupt the thought process of who might have leaked our first meeting, I started with this.

"Gentlemen, at the risk of breaking your train of thought, I should also mention I had an intruder at my home late last evening. He showed up while I was watching the 11 o'clock news on the television. He showed up in spite of the surveillance of my home from the automobile next door."

"Oh, no!" Mr. Hammond exclaimed. "What happened? Did he threaten you or your family?"

"I let him in because he was well-dressed, and I thought he had seen the light on and was asking for directions."

"Was he at all threatening or impolite? Asked Dr. Clemson.

"Yes! You might say that. His first action as he came into our kitchen was to wave a pistol in my face and demand the specifications for the heat-seeking missile our company is in the process of developing and perfecting."

"Good god, Ramsgrund, what did you do? Did you have anything to show the intruder, so he would leave you alone?"

"No, Mr. Hammond. I make it a point of never bringing anything classified home with me, so I had to dissuade him."

"And just how did you dissuade him, Ramsgrund?"

"He decided to commit suicide."

"What?" Both gentlemen exclaimed in unison. **"How the devil did that happen?"** Cried Mr. Hammond.

"What the hell are you talking about? Shouted Dr. Clemson

"I will convey to you exactly what happened in a concise, unemotional, and factual tone.

"When he entered our home, he brandished a pistol in my face and made his demands for the engineering plans for the heat-seeking missile.

"I tried to reason with him, but he had a nervous facial twitch, and his eyes kept jumping from object to object in my kitchen.

"I also noticed a blanching of his trigger finger from time to time.

"After his loud demands, my family heard his ramblings and started to come down the stairs directly into our kitchen.

"I certainly couldn't have some kind of a madman under duress waving around a loaded pistol anywhere near my family."

At that point, Dr. Clemson dropped all pretense of proper etiquette and yelled in a firm voice.

"Dear God, Ramsgrund, what did you do?"

"Well, at this point, he was regurgitating some old anti-Semitic tropes about how all Jews ought to be euthanized.

"As he turned to see who was coming down the stairs, he was distracted enough for me to grab the arm holding his firearm.

"I wrenched his arm back and placed the muzzle of the pistol under his chin with my thumb over his trigger finger.

"At this time, I encouraged him in the strongest terms not to use any further anti-Semitic language in my home ever again."

Mr. Hammond then asked calmly, subduedly, and with a very perplexed look on his face: What did the intruder do next?

"He complied with my request. First, he gave me the name of the suspicious guard in my office space, whose name was Schroder. Then he promised to never use anti-Semitic language in my home again by immediately committing suicide. He suddenly reached up with his left hand and tried to pull my elbow down and out of the way of his body – thus discharging his firearm.

"Most of his brains wound up on my ceiling, with the top of his head bouncing off the ceiling and landing on the floor beside his body. It made quite a mess for Ilsa and Greta to clean up. There was blood, bits of brain, and flesh with part of his hair, everywhere."

Both Dr. Clemson and Mr. Hammond were aghast. The blood drained from their faces.

Dr. Clemson covered his mouth with his hand and asked, "What did the police say when you notified them?"

"That is an interesting question, doctor.

"In Germany, for the past ten years or so, for a Jew to call the police would bring nothing but troubling questions for the family. The Gestapo would certainly interrogate the family in the harshest possible way, and the result could well be a concentration or death camp for the family.

"My God, Ramsgrund, this isn't the wild west or Nazi Germany! Our neighbors and police are small-town America!"

"That is the specific reason I thought it best not to call the local authorities. I felt our company would not appreciate the notoriety or the reason for my home being invaded. I understand the necessity of keeping the heat-seeking missile secret."

Mr. Hammond commented, "So, Ramsgrund, may I ask**, what the hell happened to the intruder's remains?"**

"Of course. After my wife and daughter cleaned up all the blood and gore, we wrapped what was left of his bloody head in a towel and placed him in the trunk of his automobile."

"You what! Where is the car, Ramsgrund?" Cried Mr. Hammond.

"I drove his late model Mercedes to the back parking lot of a local restaurant where it should be found in a few days because of the smell of the intruder's rotting flesh."

It took Dr. Clemson and Mr. Hammond a couple of minutes to understand exactly what had happened. You could tell they were considering all the possible ramifications to the company and to the missile project.

Mr. Hammond asked a final question while slightly shaking his head.

"Are you sure nothing on the towel or in the car would lead the authorities to you or our company?"

"Positive! No one saw me drop off the automobile. My wife picked me up quite a way distant from the parking lot."

Chapter 10

An Unsettling Development

For security protocol, no one ever comes into my office or lab area unannounced. It was a total surprise to me when I looked up from the calculations for the speed and direction of the heat-seeking missile I was working on to see a well-dressed gentleman standing next to and towering over me.

He looked to be almost six feet tall with an expensive well-fitted suit and highly polished shoes. He had a bit of a pale complexion with florid-looking cheeks. He was just a little too close to me for comfort.

I was startled and stood and asked what I thought to be an appropriate question. I stood between the tall gentleman and my work so none of my work was visible to him.

"May I help you?"

"I hope so," replied the well-appointed man in a suit looking up at me.

"Please sit down, Mr. Ramsgrund."

He extended his hand and introduced himself. I placed a trade magazine over calculations for the missile.

"I am agent Colyard Johnsen from the criminal branch of the Federal Bureau of Investigation.

"I attended our first meeting in Mr. Hammond's office a few days ago."

"Of course, Mr. Johnsen. Let me get you a chair, and we can talk here privately."

"If you don't mind, Ramsgrund, I would prefer we talk in a separate conference room for security reasons."

"I have no objections. I should mention that an intruder entered my home without resistance from the agent parked in my neighbor's drive next door.

"I understand, Ramsgrund; what do you suggest?"

"Let me lock up these plans in a secure drawer.

"Perhaps we could walk outside. I'm pretty sure there are no listening devices in the gardens."

As we walked along the walkway leading out to the parking lot, there were some tables and benches for the employees to sit and have lunch or take breaks in the nice weather. It was cool but bright and sunny, with just a few wispy clouds streaking across the horizon.

A couple of people were smoking and having a discussion at the first table we came across, so we kept walking until I was sure no one could hear us.

"What would you like to know, Mr. Johnsen?"

We sat opposite each other under a willow tree a bit away from the upper parking lot for the plant.

"What the hell happened to result in the murder of the letter-writing suspect in your kitchen last week?"

"Mr. Johnsen," I began.

"First, it was not my desire for this individual to commit suicide in my home.

It occurred to me that Mr. Johnsen was acknowledging that the letter writer was the intruder. I found that assumption interesting.

"The criminal entered my kitchen, stuck a pistol in my face, and threatened my family and me. It looked like he was about to shoot a member of my family or me if I didn't turn over certain documents related to my work at the office. His trigger finger was blanching, and he seemed very nervous. His eyes were darting around the room.

"Second, there was no 'murder'!

"An intruder came into my home in the nighttime to rob me and threaten my family with bodily harm!

"As you may know, the documents I have been developing with the engineering team are sensitive, classified, and highly secret.

"As I attempted to disarm the criminal, he decided to pull the trigger on his pistol as I was attempting to wrench it away from him.

"As he struggled to control the weapon, he was mumbling some unflattering remarks about my religion.

"To me, it was obvious that he found himself in a very difficult situation. My guess is that he considered suicide the best way out."

"I don't understand, Ramsgrund, why you were not able to disarm him and hold him until help arrived?"

"What help?"

"Was I supposed to wait until he shot my wife or daughter while I waited for the FBI or local police to come to our home?

"I have dealt with this criminal element before. These are the same type of criminals who took over my homeland in the 1930s.

"I couldn't afford to let this hoodlum think he had the advantage for another second.

"At the time, my actions were somewhat limited by the intruder's threatening and menacing waving of his pistol in my face and toward my family."

"Why didn't you try to reason with him?"

"After his anti-Semitic diatribe, I knew there was no use in trying to talk him into any reasonable course of action. He was dedicated to getting the plans for the missile or die trying."

The FBI agent's reply stunned me.

"So, you executed him in cold blood!"

"Aren't you listening to me, Agent Johnsen?"

"Yes! And I'm afraid I will have to take you into custody until we can sort this murder out."

I felt like yelling at him, but I replied in a calm and thoughtful manner. As he reached for a set of handcuffs, I thought I had better warn him.

"Agent, I do not recommend you try to restrain me. I will cooperate with your wishes and go with you quietly."

But my suggestion and calm demeanor weren't good enough for the agent. He attempted to spin me around by grabbing my wrist with the idea of placing me in restraints.

I complied by turning around quickly. As my heel spun on the turf, my elbow caught him squarely on the chin. I could hear and feel the body of the mandible fracture. *Thank you, Hitler Youth Camp!*

I grabbed his handcuffs, placed them on the agent, and locked them behind his back.

Folks from some at the nearby tables looked over with stunned and surprised looks on their questioning faces.

Agent Johnson had a very bewildered look and was mumbling something about how this action confirmed my guilt.

I spoke to him through clenched teeth.

"Sir, who do you think you are?

"Why would you even consider arresting an employee of this great corporation with no warrant, pretext, or reason?"

He was struggling with the hand restraints, and I could tell he was in pain. But then he mumbled, "You dirty Jew, you'll pay for this."

Wow! He tipped his hand. It was my second clue that he was no federal agent.

My first clue was his ability to approach my desk with my copy of plans for the Sidewinder Missile spread out in plain sight; in addition to his comment about the letter-writer.

"Sir!" I attempted to stay civil, so I replied in a quiet tone but loud enough for nearby onlookers to understand. **"I think it might be time to visit our company's security office."**

Chapter 11

A More Serious Development

The folks in Mr. Hammond's office were quite surprised when I dragged in Agent Johnsen. Unfortunately for the agent, Mr. Hammond quickly determined that although his credentials were authentic, he wasn't Agent Colyard Johnsen.

A quick check with the Boston office of the FBI proved that Agent Johnsen was working for the Federal Bureau of Investigation, but out of their Phoenix office and had never been assigned to an office in New England.

I asked Mr. Hammond what I thought to be a legitimate question.

"What should we do with this imposter?"

Mr. Hammond replied.

"Since he is in obvious pain and bleeding from the mouth, he needs immediate medical care."

"Yes. I might have broken a few teeth in addition to his lower jaw when my elbow struck him in the face."

"I will have one of our security guards take him to a local hospital and watch him until he can be turned over to the FBI."

"Mr. Hammond, could I have a word in private with you?"

"Okay, let me have my assistant watch our charlatan in a locked room while we step outside in the hall. "As we stepped out into the hall, Mr. Hammond asked: "What is it, Ramsgrund; are you feeling guilty for discovering and injuring this con artist?"

"Not at all, sir. I'm just not sure of some of the guards here at the plant."

"What are you talking about?"

"When I was struggling with the intruder in my home, just before he committed suicide, I demanded to know who his contact was at the plant."

"Did he tell you?"

"In a whimpering tone, he whispered a name: 'Schroder, the guard'."

"That name doesn't sound familiar to me," replied Mr. Hammond. "I will ask our head security guard if he knows this particular officer. Wait while I get him on the phone."

I followed the security chief back into his office while he got the head guard on the phone. Hammond didn't look happy when he cradled the phone.

"The intruder must have been mistaken, Ramsgrund. We have no one by that name on our guard list."

I handed Mr. Hammond a paper note.

"Here is the license plate number of the guard who probably left the second threatening note on my work desk."

"How the dickens did you get this?"

"I followed him as he hurriedly left my office right after I read the note. He acted suspiciously when I confronted him, so I chased after him out to the 'C' parking lot. This is the plate number of the automobile he was driving as he sped away."

"Thank you, Ramsgrund. You are amazing. You have caught an FBI imposter and discovered a possible charlatan working in our security department.

"In addition, you were able to 'disable' an intruder who was determined to do you harm and obtain corporate secrets."

"I am going to turn our imposter agent directly over to the FBI. They can handle his injuries and prosecution.

"I will also turn over the plate number you have given me. The FBI needs to follow up on our fraudulent guard. This is a serious security breach requiring a complete review of our procedures."

As I was about to leave and return to my desk, the woman behind the bunker-like office in the front stopped me. I was thanking Mr. Hammond for trusting in me and believing in my work on the new missile.

"Sir, you have a phone call."

I wasn't sure if she was addressing me or Mr. Hammond.

I raised my eyebrows and pointed to myself.

"Yes, sir. It is your daughter's school."

I ducked back into Mr. Hammond's office, asking, "Can I take the call in here?"

"Of course, Ramsgrund. Use my desk in here." He ushered me into his private office.

I picked up the phone with a little trepidation.

I was hoping my daughter hadn't acted inappropriately in her classes.

I decided to appear positive: "Good afternoon, this is Jenz Ramsgrund!"

"Good afternoon, Mr. Ramsgrund. This is Stacy in the principal's office at Sudbury High School."

"What can I do for you, Ms. Stacy? Is Greta doing, okay?"

"Well, we have a problem here, Mr. Ramsgrund."

"Has Greta been acting up in class or been impolite to any of her instructors?"

"Oh, no, Mr. Ramsgrund. Nothing like that. I was just calling to see if she might be with you."

"No, she is not with me. She should be in school at this time of day! Has she skipped any classes?"

"We tried your home, and your wife said she should be in school, but we can't locate your daughter. She was here for the opening pledge of allegiance and her first class, but she missed the rest of her classes today.

"One of her friends here said someone had come into the school and had given your daughter a note saying her mom was ill.

"However, when we called your wife, she said she had not been ill and was feeling fine.

"Do you know anything about this, Mr. Ramsgrund?"

"No. I don't think Greta would leave the school with a complete stranger. How would she get home?"

"Please make sure she is not in the school somewhere. I will call my wife and notify the local police. Please call my home or work with any information you might come across."

"Of course, Mr. Ramsgrund!" "Thanks for notifying me right away, Ms. Stacy; Goodbye."

Chapter 12

Greta is Missing

Mr. Hammond's query was immediate. "Ramsgrund, what's going on?"

"That was my daughter's school. It seems they cannot locate her, and she has missed some classes.

"Someone came to the school this morning and gave Greta a note indicating my wife, Ilsa, was ill. Since my wife is fine, the note and delivery of the note were most likely fraudulent."

"I am very sorry, Ramsgrund. Do you think your daughter's disappearance has anything to do with our difficulties here at the plant?"

"I'm not sure yet, Mr. Hammond. But it appears she was intentionally taken from her school."

"This is very disconcerting, Ramsgrund. We will do everything we can at Raytheon to secure her safety and return her to your home. My first call will be to the local police and our Boston office of the Federal Bureau of Investigation."

"Thank you, Mr. Hammond. I may need a few days off from my office in order to locate her and bring her home."

"What will you do, Ramsgrund? I don't recommend you interfere with police or FBI investigation."

"I'm not sure how familiar you are, Mr. Hammond, with my service in Germany before I came to this country."

"Yes, I know you worked at the rocket base in Peenemünde in northern Germany. Your work here on the Sidewinder heat seeking missile has been very helpful."

"Very true, and thank you, Mr. Hammond. That is where I learned many skills that will help develop offensive and defensive weapons for America's aircraft. But did you also realize I was a Lieutenant in the Schutzstaffel?"

"What is the devil is the Schutzstaffel, Ramsgrund?"

"This is an organization formed by a criminal, Heinrich Himmler, and also known as the SS. This group of criminals brought sorrow and tribulation to many thousands even millions of my countrymen.

"The misery and heartache brought on by Himmler and his henchmen to millions of my fellow Jewish and non-Jewish residents of Germany, Poland, and the other captured territories are incalculable.

"The world will never know the extent of our loss. We will never be able to know how many inventers, composers, engineers, or accountants were lost to the crematoriums.

"When this criminal, Himmler, was captured trying to flee the Reich, he took the cowardly way out and crushed a cyanide capsule between his molars and committed suicide. He was dead within twenty minutes.

"However, my time in Hitler Youth Camp and in the SS organization was not wasted. My colleague, Ezekiel Levin, and I were instrumental in saving many Jews from the Gestapo and the labor camps.

"In addition, and very importantly, we learned a skill set that will help us bring these criminal kidnappers to justice and secure the release of my daughter."

"Where will you start?"

"I have already started to develop a strategy in my thoughts. I will finish my methods of dealing with these criminals this evening with my wife, Ilsa."

"Please take as much time as you need from your work here at the plant. It is certainly in the company's interest to apprehend and put away these criminals. Our plans for the Sidewinder do not need further interruptions or delays. Our contract requires a working prototype by the end of next year.

"I understand fully, Mr. Hammond, and appreciate your letting me take some time to find my daughter.

"I will start this afternoon on my way home. If any of the administrators are still in the school, I will question them to find out any additional information they may have about Greta's day.

"It would be helpful if you could provide me with two pieces of information."

"Of course, Ramsgrund. What do you need?"

"I would need the address of the FBI office that took our imposter, Mr. Colyard Johnsen, and the address for the license registration I provided to you for the possible phony guard."

"Of course, Ramsgrund. I will provide them both for you before you leave this afternoon. Please, be careful in your search for your daughter. We do know these people are dangerous, and now we know the lengths to which they will go to get our secrets for this missile."

I spent about forty-five minutes getting my office shut down for my possible absence from work for a few days or weeks. I just wasn't quite sure how long it would take me to track down Greta's kidnappers.

I had so many concerns swirling through my mind. I needed the shortest route to the criminals who took my daughter. I knew she would be distressed, but perhaps not too panicked after what she had been through in Germany.

I hoped the kidnappers were smart enough not to hurt Greta. They really had no idea what they had gotten into or what was coming for them, once I was on to them.

I phoned Zeke to see if he could meet at my home at dinner time to help me get my thoughts organized on what to do first. He offered to take some time off from work to help me track down the criminals.

I notified my immediate boss, Jerry Lobell, of the situation, and he said he would notify Dr. Clemson, head of avionics, and bring him up-to-date on the ongoing investigation.

I emphasized that it was important not to notify the press of any kidnapping. I wanted the element of surprise on my side once I found these criminals.

Chapter 13

Ezekiel Comes to a Strategy Meeting

None of the administrators in Sudbury High School had any idea what could have happened to Greta. They had a vague description from one of the students who had seen the man who delivered the note.

Greta's girlfriend, Samantha, said he was about five feet eight inches tall with a muscular build and jet-black hair. She also indicated he spoke with a strong accent, but she couldn't place where the note-giver was from.

When I arrived home, Ezekiel called. He mentioned he was bringing his family and a couple of pizzas over for our dinner. Our conversation was direct and frank, and from the heart.

Ezekiel, as always, was thoughtful and caring.

"You know, Jenz. These kidnappers probably have no idea whom they are dealing with. You and I both know what Greta went through when attacked by the Gestapo. She had been brutalized, almost raped, and saw her father beaten in their own home in Nordhausen.

"In addition, you have seen how resourceful she was when she disguised herself as your male aide in order to flee the Reich."

"I realize that, Zeke. It's just that, as her stepfather, I am charged with keeping her safe, and I haven't done that. I thought America would be much different from the last few years of terror and uncertainty in Germany."

"America **is** very different, Jenz. Let's think logically about how we will get her back home. Are you going to wait until you hear from the kidnappers?"

"Absolutely not! I will go right after them starting this evening."

Ezekiel asked. "Jenz, how are you going to start looking for her this evening?"

"The school administrator at Greta's school gave me her girlfriend's telephone number. She is the one that actually met the man who delivered the note meant for Greta. I'm going to call her home right after dinner before it gets too late and see if I can get a more accurate description of the note-giving intruder."

I called Samantha right after we finished our pizza. I noticed it was hard for Ilsa, Adiya, and Chasha to eat very much; Zeke and I had to finish the last few slices of pizza on our own.

When I was able to get Samantha on the phone, I started to question her directly.

"Samantha, this is Mr. Ramsgrund, Greta's father. Is there anything further you could tell me about the man who delivered the note to you intended for Greta? Even small details would be helpful."

"Well, Mr. Ramsgrund, he seemed a little nervous and ill at ease. I could tell he didn't belong in the school."

"Were there any distinguishing characteristics about this man that stood out in your mind?"

"He was pretty tall; perhaps five feet eight or ten inches tall. He also had very white skin, almost like he had never been out in the sun. His hair, however, was jet-black with just a touch of grey around the temples. He was quite old, possibly around forty."

"How was he dressed, Samantha?"

"His trousers and sports jacket were narrow-cut. His clothes almost seemed too small for him."

"Anything else you can think of, Samantha? Did he have an accent?"

"Yes, he did have an accent, but I really couldn't place where he might have been from."

"Did he speak or sound at all like this: *Sprichst du Deutsch, Liebchen?*"

"A little like that, but I am taking an afterschool elective in Russian. His accent was almost a cross between English and Russian."

"Interesting," I replied. "Is there anything else you could tell me? Could you describe any distinguishing facial features or the type and color of his automobile?"

"He had a roundish face with a short stubby neck. He also had a line or perhaps an old scar from his right eye almost to his right ear lobe. I'm sorry, but I never saw his car. Oh, he was also in need of a shave. He looked quite stubbly."

"Excellent, Samantha. You have given me a lot to consider and a very concise description."

"Well, I hope I have been helpful, Mr. Ramsgrund. My meeting with this stranger was very brief. All he said was to 'please give this note to Greta Ramsgrund. It concerns her mother.' Greta is a nice friend."

"Yes. Very helpful, Samantha. Thank you, and good night."

Ezekiel had written down everything Samantha told me as she was describing the unknown intruder.

"Zeke, we now have a fairly decent description of the man we need to locate."

"Yes." Replied Zeke. "I will meet you at the school when it opens early tomorrow. I would like to know if we can get a description of the man's automobile or even a license number."

"Thanks, Zeke. And thanks for the moral support of Adiya and Chasha. Also, thanks for the elegant pizza dinner."

Just then, the phone rang.

"Mr. Ramsgrund?"

"Yes."

"This is Mr. Hammond's secretary, Stella."

"Hi, Stella. What can I do for you?"

"Mr. Hammond asked me to give you the address for the registration number you had given him for a Mr. Schroder."

"Yes. Thank you, Stella."

"Mr. Schroder lives on 2031 Saint John Street, in Jamacia Plane."

"Thank you very much, Stella. You have been most helpful.

Chapter 14

⇒∘⧉∘⇐

A Meeting at Sudbury High School

A cold late fall wind whistled across the meadow behind the barn the next morning. There were a few wind-blown flakes of early snow in the offing. I tightened my coat against the intrusiveness of the coming winter.

Unfortunately, my mood matched the weather. I blamed myself for underestimating the length these criminals would go to obtain the secrets of the Sidewinder program. My primary responsibility was protecting my family, and I needed to do better.

It was my job to look after and protect my stepdaughter, and I had failed her. My failure heightened and steeled my resolve to get her back safely and bring unholy punishment against the perpetrators.

As I approached the high school, I noticed one of the two Sudbury police vehicles parked at the entrance of the parking area. The school administration, or perhaps the security office at Raytheon, had notified the local authorities.

True to his word, Zeke was already sitting outside the principal's office and greeted me as I walked in.

"Did you sleep okay, Jenz?"

"I tried, but I kept thinking about Greta and how she was handling her kidnappers and how they were holding her against her will, including whatever they might try to do to her."

Zeke tried to be reassuring.

"Greta might be a young woman, Jenz, but she is hardly defenseless. She has seen enough and been through enough in Germany to be probably pretty much okay, no matter what these criminals attempt to throw at her."

"You're probably right, Zeke. But I couldn't feel closer to her if she were my own flesh and blood. I must look out for her since her dad is still in the Fatherland."

"Don't blame yourself for her kidnapping. These criminals have proven they will stop at nothing to get the secrets you are working on at the plant."

Just then, the school secretary came out and asked for Zeke and me to come in and talk with the school principal.

"Good morning, Mr. Ramsgrund?"

"Yes. Good morning. Are you Ms. Stacy?"

"Yes."

"Thanks for seeing us early, before school starts. This is my friend and colleague, Dr. Ezekiel Leven."

"Good morning, sir. Please come right this way."

We were ushered into Mr. Jacobson's office, the principal of Sudbury High School.

"Mr. Jacobson, this is Greta's father, Mr. Jenz Ramsgrund, and his colleague, Dr. Ezekiel Levin."

"Thanks for meeting with us, Mr. Jacobson; Ezekiel, my wife, and I are very worried for Greta's safety. Have you any idea who came into the school yesterday to take her?"

"No first-hand knowledge, Mr. Ramsgrund. However, I will let you speak to our maintenance supervisor, Mr. Evans. He is quite knowledgeable about the coming and going of people coming into the school during off hours. We are considering having a sign-in process for all visitors, but we just haven't seen the need for it until this serious 'incident' came up yesterday.

"I will tell you both that your daughters seem to be acclimating pretty well here at SHS. The first few months of transition seemed a bit difficult for them, but I have recently had excellent reports from their teachers."

Mr. Evans was paged and promptly came into the principal's office. He seemed surprised to see so many of us in the office so early but immediately asked a question.

"What can I do for you, Principal Jacobson?"

"Evans, this is Mr. Ramsgrund, whose daughter, Greta, was lured away from our school yesterday, and his colleague, Dr. Leven. Dr. Leven also has a daughter, Chasha, here at the high school.

"Is there anything you could tell us about the circumstances of her disappearance from our school yesterday morning?"

"Well, I am not sure if this would help, Mr. Jacobson, but my staff and I make a habit of jotting down the license number of all automobiles that come into the school after the beginning of classes. We ignore all the cars that drop off or pick up students at the beginning and end of the day.

"If you would like, I could check with my staff and get a list of those license registration numbers."

"Please do; immediately, if you are able!"

"I will retrieve the list from my office and return directly."

Mr. Evans was gone less than five minutes. A local police officer came into the office while we were waiting for the maintenance man to return.

He introduced himself as Officer Dan Auberon.

"Good morning, folks. I am here as the local police support to investigate and help locate the student missing from your school yesterday. In addition, our office has notified the Federal Bureau of Investigation."

Introductions were made as Mr. Evans returned from his office.

"Gentlemen, I'm sorry, but we only had five automobiles come into our school yesterday during school hours that were not delivering or picking up students. One of them could be the automobile of the man who lured the student out of her classroom, but I have no idea which one or if we missed him altogether."

He gave the list to Mr. Jacobson.

"Thank you, Evans. Excellent!"

Mr. Jacobson remarked, "We just installed a new copy machine in the office. Let me make a copy for our local police."

"If it wouldn't be too much trouble," I spoke up. "Could I also have a copy to see if anything looks familiar to me?"

I not only wanted to see if any of the license numbers matched the plate number I had seen leaving the Raytheon lot, but I wanted an immediate follow-up on any suspicious numbers.

"Not at all, Mr. Ramsgrund. Perhaps Officer Auberon could find out the addresses that match the license numbers."

"Of course, Jacobson. However, I will have to call in the numbers from my squad car in order for my office to access the main office records for the addresses. The record office should also give the make, model, color, and year of the automobiles. It will take up to half an hour for a telephone expedited search by the administrator."

"Thanks, Officer. In the interim, I will make an announcement over the speaker system, since the school day has begun, for anyone who might have seen or know anything about this abduction. I will have them come immediately to the principal's office."

Two students came to the office. Samantha, Greta's friend whom I had talked with last evening, and another freshman student who thought she saw Greta leave in a dark brown or black four-door sedan.

Officer Auberon returned with a little news.

"Gentlemen, four of the five license numbers belong to Sudbury residents. The only one registered out of Sudbury is an automobile registered to a resident of Medford: Mrs. Jerome E. Willigan, who lives at 2490 Mystic Valley Parkway."

"Since it was a male who picked up your daughter, Mr. Ramsgrund, I'm not sure if this list is of any help."

"Thanks, Officer Auberon. Any information on the kidnapping of my daughter is, I'm sure, helpful.

"How will you follow up on the information, officer?"

"Oh, we will call the local police in Medford and have them question Mrs. Willigan."

"Thanks, officer. Please let me know immediately if you have any further information."

Zeke and I talked after we got to my car.

"What do you think, Jenz?"

"Officer Auberon was very helpful, but I am going directly to the address listed for the registration and will do a little questioning on my own.

"Also, I am going to the address provided to me from my office for the guard, Schroder. I think it might be in the same area of this address. He was possibly involved with leaving me notes in my office and may have something to do with intimidating my family and kidnapping Greta."

"Would you mind a little company, Jenz?"

"No! I would welcome it. I am quite worried about what might be happening to my daughter. Do you remember she was assaulted in her own home in Nordhausen?"

"Of course, I remember, Jenz. Let's hope the perpetrators are smart enough not to try anything before they contact you for information on the plans for the work you are doing at Raytheon."

"My goal, Ezekiel, is to surprise the criminals and contact them before they can do anything that may harm Greta. I am very worried for her safety.

"The address that Stella from the security office provided was in a section of Boston. I am just not too familiar with that area. The other address is in Medford. I am not sure which is closer.

"Ezekiel sighed and said, "Let's take a ride."

Chapter 15

Greta's Immediate Situation

From the moment she had been forced into the boot of the Mercedes sedan, Greta had been thinking of ways to get out of her confining prison. She felt angry toward her abductor, but she knew what was in store for him whenever Jenz caught up to him.

She estimated it must have been about an hour before they came to a complete stop. There was a lot of traffic and stopping and starting the vehicle, so she thought they must be somewhere in a city.

After the car stopped moving, the automobile slowly went into reverse. A garage door could be heard closing, and someone banged on the trunk. Greta could hear nothing but her own breathing. Slowly the trunk was unlatched.

Greta grabbed a tire iron and was ready to swing it at the first face to appear in the trunk opening.

Instead, a pistol was shown through the half-opened trunk, and a black hood was tossed in.

A man shouted at her. **"Put this hood over your head and come out slowly."**

Greta did as she was instructed but forced her little finger, which had a very sharp fingernail, through the cloth in order to get a glimpse of whoever had abducted her.

As she was slowly climbing out of the trunk, strong hands grabbed her and jerked her out but left her standing.

The garage had windows across the top, and Greta got a look at a pizza shop across the street.

"Where are we?" she asked.

"None of your business, kid!" Was the retort of a heavily accented voice.

Greta knew the accent wasn't German, but she was trying to figure out the origin; it almost sounded Russian. She needed more conversation to place the correct region for the dialect origination, so she asked another rather innocent question.

"Why have you taken me?

Slap!

The kidnapper, with a heavy accent, slapped her across the face. With the hood on, she didn't see it coming. She went down on her knees.

"Ouch!" cried Greta. "You will be very sorry you struck me."

"We will do much more than that if your father is not cooperative!" The kidnapper exclaimed.

Greta seemed calm and stood upright after her traumatic slap. She guessed that his accent was from Eastern Poland or Russia. The other kidnapper sounded very Russian with a German accent. She wanted to draw him out more and test for any vulnerabilities.

She wasn't planning on being too difficult or confrontational, but she wanted to let the kidnappers know they weren't totally in control.

"I'm hungry and thirsty. When are you planning on feeding me? I missed lunch, and it must be close to dinner time."

"Jeeze, Demetri, what are we going to feed her?"

"Do not use any names! A pizza from down the street ought to hold this little witch until we hear from her father.

"In the meantime, we will lock her in the cellar. Tied up and with the hood covering her eyes, she won't be going anywhere. There is no exit from the cellar, and the windows are too small for escape.

"We will blindfold her when she eats so she will not be able to recognize us."

"Jeeze, Demetri. You've thought of everything."

Demetri just rolled his eyes. He decided not to be confrontational about his thuggish companion using his first name again in front of their hostage.

"Just put her in the chair in the cellar and lock the door. Feel free to slap her around, if she gets uncooperative."

"Yes, boss! Should I tie her to the chair?"

"It won't be necessary. Keep her hands tied and her hood on. She will be cooperative, or she won't get fed!

"Let her use the bathroom only if she really needs it. This one could be slippery. Her accent tells me she could well be a refugee from the war."

Chapter 16

Imprisoned!

Suddenly, Greta felt very alone. Her hands were tied and connected with a short length of rope behind her back, a black hood covered her head, and when the lights were turned off in the cellar, she could see absolutely nothing.

The small hole she had made in her hood was not aligned with her vision because of the slap from the kidnapper. There was very little light coming in the windows because, by now, it was totally dark outside.

For the first time since being abducted, Greta felt very alone. Her primary concern was wanting to move around. She didn't want to move around without seeing what was around her in the cellar.

Then she had an idea.

If I could get my hands under my backside and wiggle my legs out, I could get my hands in front of me, and I could remove my hood. Perhaps, if I could see how my hands are bound, perhaps I could untie them with my mouth and the fingers of my other hand.

She had to wiggle around on her backside on the cement cellar floor to wiggle her legs through the loop of the short rope that tied her hands behind her back. The whole gymnastic experience took almost thirty minutes.

With her hands in front of her, she could remove her hood and, with difficulty, see her surroundings by the faint light coming from the outside streetlights through the cellar windows.

After a few more minutes, she could untie her left wrist by pulling the knot with her teeth and right-hand fingers.

Her eyes were growing accustomed to the dim light, and she was able to see her way around the cellar.

Greta got out of the chair, stretched her legs a bit, took a short walk around the cellar, and took in everything she could identify: pipes, valves, electrical wiring, and what looked like an electrical fuse box.

Just as she was about to take another more careful tour around the cellar, she heard the upstairs door open, and the cellar light snapped on.

She quickly returned to her chair, re-tied the left wrist loosely but in front of her, and replaced the black hood over her head.

The not-so-smart kidnapper came down the stairs, placed a box with a still-warm pizza in her lap, and removed her hood.

"Here, you little witch, this ought to hold you for a while."

Greta decided to challenge the thug. **"Where have you taken me?"**

"That, young lady, you will never know. However, if your father is smart, you should be home in a few days."

Greta decided to turn up the heat and the rhetoric.

"You stupid thugs! You will be very sorry when my father gets a hold of you!"

"Your father will never find you unless he cooperates with us, little girl, so shut up and eat your pizza before I put your hood back on."

"You thugs don't scare me!" His breath had a strong garlic smell, and his clothing stank of cigarette smoke. She didn't want him getting his smoke-stained fingers near her pizza.

The thug's behavior brought back very stark memories of her assault by the Gestapo in her home in Nordhausen. She didn't want this scum anywhere near her.

She thought about her father. Was he trapped in the Russian part of Germany? She hoped and prayed he was okay.

She calmed down a bit and started eating a slice of plain pizza.

The kidnapper didn't seem to notice Greta's hands were tied in front of her, and he left her eating her pizza without covering her eyes.

His parting words as he ascended the cellar stairs: **"Behave yourself, girlie, or there will be trouble. I will be just upstairs having supper with my friends who brought you here. They would not hesitate to get rough with you if you do not cooperate."** He gave Greta a nasty smile as he ascended the stairs.

Greta quickly finished her pizza and looked around the cellar to see what trouble she could find.

Looking around the back wall of the cellar, she found a workbench with various tools. Jenz had taught her the basics of carpentry, so she knew what she was looking for.

The dim gloom of the cellar matched her mood. She was tired of dealing with these criminals and wanted a plan for escape.

Chapter 17

Greta's Ingenuity

It wasn't that Greta necessarily wanted to cause trouble for herself, but if she could bring trouble, discomfort, or carnage to those who had kidnapped her and forced her into the trunk of their car, then into this dank cellar, well, she would not hesitate to do it.

At first glance, she thought about cutting off the power to the house. However, the thugs could easily come down and restore the power at the fuse box. They might slap her around after that and tie her up tighter and probably tight to the chair.

She looked around the dimly lit cellar and came to the pipe from the street that carried the natural gas to the furnace and hot water heater. If she could fill the cellar with gas, there could be a fire or explosion, which would seriously interrupt the kidnapper's plans.

Greta felt she might be able to squeeze through one of the cellar windows. She would have to find some way of getting up near the narrow windows to have any hope of escaping quickly once the gas started to flow into the cellar.

If she could disconnect the gas line and fill the cellar with gas, she needed a quick and foolproof method of escape.

She tried standing on a chair to gain access to one of the cellar windows. Although the window opening was narrow, she thought she could squeeze through with a little effort. She unlatched and opened the window. She could see the street from her perch on the chair and saw the red reflection of the pizza sign on the sidewalk. With a little incentive, like gas filling the cellar, she was sure she could get quickly out through the cellar window.

Greta went back to the workbench and looked for an adjustable wrench. She couldn't find exactly what she was looking for but found a locking pair of plyers. *"I think dad called these channel locks."*

"These should work," she whispered to herself. "Now I need to find a valve to disconnect."

At the junction of the gas furnace, a T-joint led gas to the hot water heater. Just before the hot water heater, there was another short T-joint. One end of the T-joint led to the hot water heater, the other end short end was capped with a threaded removable cap. This dead-end short pipe was probably used to collect condensation from the incoming gas.

"If I can remove the cap on the lower end of the gas pipe, the gas should flow freely into the cellar."

Just then, the cellar door opened, and the light snapped on. Greta placed the locking plyers under the hot water heater, scrambled back to her chair, and retied her left wrist to the short length of rope. She hopped the locking plyers were far enough under the hot water heater to be out of sight.

The thug with the cigarette-smoked hands called down as he descended the stairs. **"I hope you have been good, girlie; I don't want to have to slap you around to make you good."**

"You are already in big trouble, you thug. Why would you want to get into more trouble?"

"You're the one in trouble, girlie. If your father doesn't bring us what we need for our country, he will never see you again."

Just then, the phone rang in the kitchen.

The thug quickly placed a cloth-colored handkerchief in Greta's mouth and tied a short rope snugly around her head so she couldn't spit it out. He then grabbed her hood and stretched it over her head.

"Now remember girlie, no noise. If I hear any noise from the cellar, I will have to come down here and make you quiet."

"You don't frighten me, you pig." At least, that was what she was trying to say. It came out like muffled gibberish.

Chapter 18

The Hunt

The minute Office Auberon jotted down the registration address gleaned from the license plate of the automobile at Sudbury High School, many ideas came to my mind. Zeke and I discussed a list of what was most important for me in getting Greta back safely.

My priority was getting Greta back home and perhaps checked out by our local doctor. Second, I wanted to punish whoever kidnapped my daughter.

After jotting down the name and address from the maintenance supervisor, Mr. Evans, Jenz turned to Zeke and pointed to his car.

Zeke and I immediately went to a petrol station on Route 20 to fill the tank and find out how to get to the cities of Jamaica Plain and Medford, Massachusetts.

"I think they are close to or even part of Boston," Zeke commented.

"What is the fastest route to Medford and Boston?" was my question.

Zeke talked with the attendant as he was fueling up my automobile.

"Your best bet is to stay on this route until you are near Cambridge and then travel north to Medford. I will get you a map of the city and show you the best route from Medford to the Jamaica Plain section," answered the attendant.

"You will go through Watertown and Waltham, then follow the signs to Medford. Route 2 might be a help to get you to Mystic Valley

Parkway. Jamaica Plain is a bit south of the city. The maps are 15 cents, but one would help you navigate the city."

Although there was light traffic on the roadway, I didn't want to get a speeding ticket. As we got closer to the city of Boston, traffic was more congested. Unfortunately, we were caught in a bit of a rush-hour situation.

It was just getting dark by the time we found Medford.

Zeke asked what turned out to be an important question.

"Should we press on this evening to try to find this address?"

"I would like to find the address, but I agree, it might not be too good to be confrontational this evening."

Meanwhile, Jenz's wife, Ilsa, had already taken a phone call from the kidnappers.

"Mrs. Ramsgrund?"

"Yes"

"We have your daughter."

"Who is this?"

"Never mind who this is. Let me talk with your husband."

"Jenz isn't here right now. You better return Greta to her home before Jenz finds you."

"Tell your husband your daughter will be returned unharmed if he delivers a set of plans for the heat-seeking missile as he was instructed. Without those plans delivered immediately, I cannot guarantee the safety of your daughter."

Now Ilse was very angry and responded a little more forcefully than prudent.

"Unless you ensure Greta's safety and deliver her immediately, I cannot guarantee your safety!"

The call infuriated her; after hanging up, she called the local police.

The Sudbury police told her that the Boston office of the Federal Bureau of Investigation would contact her immediately.

The officer at the FBI phoned Ilse and said they would be out that afternoon to monitor her phone line.

"Mrs. Ramsgrund," the FBI officer informed her.

"These are very dangerous people that have taken your daughter. We have learned they are involved with the Russian mafia gangsters and cannot be trusted. Please do everything you are instructed to do and keep us informed. We will be monitoring your phone conversations."

"Sir," replied Ilse. "Unfortunately, these criminals have no idea what my husband is capable of if they harm Greta in any way. I should tell you; she is not a shy seventeen-year-old girl. The Gestapo had brutalized her during the war, and these thugs have no inkling whom they have taken."

"Please, Mrs. Ramsgrund, we know you are upset. Let us do our job and find your daughter."

Ilse shot back, "I hope you find them before my husband does. Good-bye."

Meanwhile, Jenz and Ezekiel slowly passed by the address on Mystic Valley Parkway in Medford.

"It looks like a large apartment complex, Jenz. Should we drop in on Mrs. Willigan? It looks a little run-down.

Meanwhile, the Sudbury police had telephoned the registered owner of the license plate observed by the janitor from Sudbury High School.

"Mrs. Jerome Willigan?"

"Yes, this is Mrs. Willigan."

"This is Officer Auberon from the Town of Sudbury police department."

"What can I do for you, Officer Auberon?"

"Are you the owner of a black Chevrolet sedan with Massachusetts plate # C574-32?"

"Why yes. Why do you ask?"

"Was your car involved with dropping off or picking up anything or anyone from the high school in Sudbury today?"

"Why no. I don't think so. To tell you the truth, my son uses the car most of the time. He thinks I'm too old to drive, even though I'm only eighty."

"Where is your son now, Mrs. Willigan?"

"Well, he lives in Revere. But he would have no reason to be out your way in Sudbury."

"Thank you, Mrs. Willigan; this is just a routine matter. Could you please give me your son's full name, address, and phone number?"

"My son is Jerry Zemanski. He lives on Harris Street, number 28, I believe, in Revere. His telephone number is RE 2-3895. I could call him and have him contact you."

"There is no need to contact him, Mrs. Willigan. This is not important enough to bother him. Thank you for the information."

As soon as Officer Auberon hung up the phone, he called the Ramsgrund residence.

"Mrs. Ramsgrund?"

"Yes."

"This is Officer Auberon from the Sudbury police station. Is Mr. Ramsgrund at home?"

"No, I'm sorry, officer, I haven't heard from him since he left this morning. He wanted to meet with the high school principal at the school. Have you heard anything about Greta?"

"The FBI has informed us they are monitoring your phone.

"I have the address and phone number of a person of interest who might have been driving the automobile that was seen at the high school earlier today. Please have your husband call me at the station as soon as possible."

Chapter 19

Clues

Zeke and I parked in the lot outside of the four well-worn brick apartment buildings making up the complex. We found the Willigan apartment by the list of occupants on the lobby floor of building three.

I didn't want to waste any time in our search for Greta, so Zeke and I entered the secured part of the lobby when someone was leaving. We knocked on the Willigan's apartment door just after the dinner hour.

"Good evening, Mrs. Willigan?"

"Yes, what can I do for you, gentlemen?"

"We are so sorry to disturb you this evening, but are you the owner of a black Chevrolet sedan?"

"Yes. But the Sudbury police already called me about this automobile. I told them my son has the car most of the time. He thinks that because I'm eighty years old, I shouldn't be driving too much. He uses the car most of the time, but I'm pretty sure he hasn't been out to Sudbury recently."

"Thanks, Mrs. Willigan. Could you tell us how to get in touch with your son?"

"Sure. But I have already given the Sudbury police all the information for Jerry. He lives nearby in Revere."

"Thanks, Mrs. Willigan; we can get the information from them."

"My son isn't in any trouble, is he?"

"I don't think so, Mrs. Willigan. We just need to clear a few things up with him."

"Oh! Thank goodness. I was afraid some of the people he associates with on the weekends might have gotten him in trouble with the police."

Zeke asked, "Who is friendly with your son, Mrs. Willigan?"

"Oh," she remarked, "It's his Russian associates he hangs around with on the weekends. During the week, he has a steady job and works hard. I just don't trust the Russians; they always seem to be shading the law."

"I'm sorry to hear that, Mrs. Willigan. Just what is it that your son does for a living?" I asked.

"Well," Mrs. Willigan replied, "From what I understand, he runs a delivery service for several different companies. Those Russians are always trying to get him to deliver packages for them. They must pay him well. He is always helping me out with the rent and groceries."

"Where is your son's place of business, Mrs. Willigan?"

"I know he works some out of his home in Revere, but his office is somewhere in Jamacia Plane. I have his office address somewhere in my desk. Let me get it for you. Yes. Here it is. He works from an office on St. John Street in Jamaica Plain. The office address is 2031 St. John Street."

"Thank you, Mrs. Willigan. You have been very helpful, and we are sorry to disturb you at the dinner hour."

"Oh, you don't disturb me! Since my husband died 10 years ago, I have been living here alone. Eating by myself gets a little sad after a while."

After Zeke and I left Mrs. Willigan's apartment, we sat in the car and discussed our next step.

"Zeke, do you think we should follow up on either the addresses for Jerry Zemanski this evening?"

"Although it is getting a little late, Jenz, we don't know what kind of danger Greta could be facing."

"Are you okay going over and driving by his office in Jamacia Plane, Zeke? If he has Greta, I don't think he would take her to his home."

"Let's head over there right now, Jenz. Traffic shouldn't be too busy by this time of night.

"I hope her kidnappers are smart enough not to move her too far away."

"I hope they are smart enough not to molest her. She can be very enterprising when left to think on her own. You remember, Zeke, how she got out of the Reich as the Allies and Russians were attacking and closing in on our country."

"Oh, I remember, Jenz. You have a very independent and bright daughter who can be dangerous to these fools who have kidnapped her."

In another city near Boston, a dangerous situation was developing.

Greta had been struggling with the locking plyers after the Russian thug had run upstairs to get the phone. She had no trouble removing the wrist ties she had retied and removed the gag.

The plyers kept slipping until she found the locking mechanism for adjusting them to the correct size for the gas cap on the drip pipe. Once the cap was removed, gas immediately started flowing into the cellar.

Greta made a little stepping ladder out of some boxes for easy egress from the cellar window. After opening the window and ensuring a quick exit for herself, she went over to the fuse box and threw the switch to cut the power.

"Now I have to get out of here fast," she said quietly to herself. She quickly climbed over the boxes and squirmed out the cellar window and closed it behind her.

She could hear shouting from upstairs as the kidnappers were swearing at each other and blaming one of the thugs, Sigi, for not securing Greta. She could hear them clomping down the stairs in the dark. Flashlight beams were crisscrossing the cellar looking for her.

The minute the Russian, Demetri, heard the word 'gas,' he ran outside to catch Jerry, who was just leaving after having some pizza with his fellow thugs.

"Jerry, hold up! The cellar had a strong gas smell; Sigi and one of the Russians went down to check on our captive and find out if there was a leak anywhere. We lost power at the same time; I hope Greta hasn't been up to mischief."

Just then, Jerry shouted, "Isn't that Greta running down the street?"

"I think you are right!" Demetri shouted back.

"If we lose her, our Russian handlers will take out their anger on us. Let's catch up to her before she gets to the next block."

Jerry accelerated his automobile quickly and stopped half a block in front of Greta. It was quite dark, with poor street lighting. Greta didn't even notice them until they jumped out of the bushes, forcibly grabbed her, and dragged her into the trunk of their automobile.

Meanwhile, Sigi, the not-too-intelligent thug, was crossing the cellar looking for the main electrical switch for the power to the house. His flashlight beam played on the front of the cellar facing the street.

"That electrical box should be near here," he remarked to his Russian companion.

"I think I found it," shouted Sigi. "But where is our captive?"

Both men saw the brilliant flash of light right after throwing the main switch on the electrical box. Neither, however, heard the clap of the thunderous explosion or felt the searing two-thousand-degree heat that burned their bodies to a crisp.

Jenz and Ezekiel were just coming into Jamacia Plane when they saw a flash of light on the horizon followed by what sounded like a clap of thunder.

"Wow, Jenz! Isn't that near the street Mrs. Willigan gave us for Jerry's office?"

You might be right, Zeke. There are emergency vehicles heading down this street behind us. I can see their flashing lights. I hope Greta isn't involved and she is safe."

The ensuing fire was quickly extinguished by the Jamaica Plane Fire Department. The City of Boston Department came as a back-up.

Zeke and I watched the proceedings with a growing crowd of onlookers from across the street. After an hour, the fire Marshall investigating the smoldering ruins exclaimed the cause was leaking gas and two male corpses were found in the cellar of the structure.

Although Zeke and I were relieved Greta wasn't among the ruins of the building, our immediate concern was, **"Where the devil is she, Zeke?"**

"Look, Jenz. We have to consider the most positive outcome. Doesn't this explosion and fire at the location of the kidnapper's office have Greta's signature all over it?"

"You could be right, Zeke! But if she has caused this conflagration and escaped, where could she be?"

At this point, Greta had been dragged from her imprisonment in the kidnapper's trunk of their automobile, drugged, and hustled onto a plane bound for Europe. Jenz and Zeke had no idea that the next time they would hear from Greta would be in an East German prison in East Berlin.

Chapter 20

A Search for Greta

The first notification of the location of my daughter came two days after frantically searching for her in the cities of Boston, Jamacia Plane and Revere, Medford, Massachusetts.

My first inkling of her whereabouts came when Ezekiel and I "questioned" Mr. Jerold Willigan at his apartment in Revere.

We knocked on his door at 7 am the next morning.

Although it took a while, a tired looking Jerry Willigan eventually opened the front door to his apartment.

"Jerry Willigan?" I asked in the friendliest possible tone I could muster.

"Yeah, who wants to know?" was his lackluster and disinterested response.

"I am Greta Ramsgrund's father."

"I don't know who you are talking about!" He shouted, as he attempted to slam the door in our face.

Fortunately, my size 14 shoe was inserted between the door and the jamb and the door bounced back open hitting Jerry in his face.

What surprised him even more was my shoulder pushing the door wide open so Zeke and I could gain entrance to his apartment. I pushed hard with my shoulder and sent him sprawling onto the floor.

I grabbed him up by the front of his shirt and threw him into a chair.

"Please, don't hurt me!" He was whimpering in a scratchy voice. You could tell we had awoken him from a sound sleep.

"We will leave you alone, Mr. Willigan, as soon as you tell us where Greta is located." Zeke informed him in a firm, but quiet tone.

"I have no idea who you are talking about!" He whimpered.

"Let us refresh your memory, Mr. Willigan." Zeke kept a smooth, yet firm tone. "You showed up two days ago and lured a young woman away from Sudbury high school on the pretense that her mother was ill. You then kidnapped her to an unknown location in Jamacia Plane. That location suffered an explosion and fire, but Greta was not in the building. She hasn't been heard from since.

"Does that refresh your memory, Jerry?" Zeke's voice was still remarkably calm.

"I don't know anything. Get out and leave me alone!" Jerry was starting to shout.

I put my finger to my lips and encourage him. "Jerry, Jerry, there is no need to shout or get excited. We are normally very peaceful men.

"However, if you don't tell us immediately where my daughter is located, I will have to use some very unpleasant techniques that had been in common use in my country, Nazi Germany."

"What techniques, I don't know anything!

"Jerry, Jerry, Jerry." I replied in a calm straight-forward manner using a thick German accent.

"During the war, in my country, the Gestapo, used inhumane techniques to elicit information from anyone they deemed an enemy of the state."

"I'm no enemy of anyone."

"Let me explain something to you, Jerry Willigen, as clearly and concisely as possible." I said this in a deep, heavily-accented German voice.

"If you do not immediately tell me where we can find my daughter, I will personally remove all of your fingers, one at a time, until you tell me all you know about my daughter's location."

I was trying to be polite, but this goon was starting to try my patents. In addition, to coffee, I hadn't had much breakfast. I could feel my blood sugar starting to sink a bit.

"Unfortunately, Jerry, we do not have a lot of time. My daughter's health and welfare pre-emps any of your creature comforts.

In one smooth motion, I grabbed his hand, jerked him to his feet, and squeezed his hand until I broke his little finger.

He let out a muffled scream.

"No, you can't!"

His voice was muffled because Zeke had covered his mouth from behind.

"Ah, I intoned in a quiet, heavily accented and sympathetic voice. Let's start with this one, it is already broken anyway! Zeke would you mind getting a sharp knife and cutting board from the kitchen?"

At that moment he fell to the floor and screamed. **"No! Please, you can't!"**

I reassured him in a firm and heavily accented voice. "Jerry, if you want, you can watch, because this is only the first. You have four fingers left to go on this hand."

"No! Please. I don't know where your daughter is!

"Then you admit you took her from Sudbury High School?"

He was whimpering and barely able to speak. He was shaking and stuttering so badly his speech was barely intelligible, but he nodded in the affirmative.

"It… was the Russians, they told me they would hurt my mother if I didn't do what I wanted."

"Speak up, Jerry. I want to make sure I understand you completely. And, we have met your mother. She is a lovely person. Ezekiel and I could never cause her any harm.

"If you tell us immediately where Greta is located, I will put your finger in ice-water and your pain will immediately go away. The finger can then be splinted and it will heal properly.

"However, if you are not truthful, your little finger will be removed and your ring finger broken immediately!"

"Please! The last I saw her she was in tied in the cellar in our office in Jamacia Plane. I have no idea where they took her after the fire."

"Excellent, Jerry. You are doing very well. You have shown good judgement in cooperating with us. My apology for breaking your finger. You will keep your fingers as long as you continue to cooperate with us."

"What more can I tell you! I don't have any idea where they took her."

He was starting to whimper again; I had to give him some encouragement so I could understand him.

"I tell you what, Jerry. You, Ezekiel, and I, are going to form a little partnership.

"What are you talking about. I already told you all I know."

He was hyperventilating.

In a firm voice I told him, "Jerry, you are going for a little ride with us. You are going to take us directly to where your friends are keeping Greta. **Now!** If you do not take us directly to her location, I will make sure you lose more than your fingers."

"Please," he shouted. We, we, turned her over to the Russians. They said they would kill us if anyone said where they were taking her. She is probably in East Berlin by now."

"What are you talking about!" I have to admit, I was a little heated. My low blood sugar had started to affect my mood.

"Tell me exactly, who took my daughter? **"Now!"**

In a whimpering, shaking voice, Jerry replied, "We had to turn her over to the Russians. The Stasi* said they would kill us if we ever disclosed that we turned her over to the Russians. In a little firmer voice I demanded, **"Exactly where did they take my daughter?"**

"I'm afraid they took her to the airport in Boston and then to Germany," whimpered Jerry.

Now he got my attention. "Are you saying the Russians took my daughter out of the country?"

Jerry replied in a timid, barely audible voice. "I am so sorry. I think they were going to take her to East Berlin.

---

*The Stasi were the most terrifying secret police in the Eastern Block. Stasi is an abbreviation for *Staatssicherheit,* State Security Service of East Germany. Essentially, the Stasi was patterned after the Russian KGB. They spread fear to the citizens of East Germany from 1950 to 1990.

Chapter 21

West Berlin, Germany – Spring 1951

Two days later, Ezekiel and I were at lunch in a quiet small restaurant near the *Tiergarten** in West Berlin. The eatery was tucked into a small shopping center but looked new and clean. The park itself was almost completely denuded of trees. Our waiter said the local population had cut down most of the trees for firewood because of a shortage of fuel and expense for coal after the war. The winter had been quite severe.

I asked the waiter, "Is there anything we should be aware of while traveling to the Eastern section of the city?"

"So far, there are no restrictions for travel between the eastern and western controlled parts of the city. This might change later if the entire eastern population part of the city wants to move to the western part of the city and away from the communist bloc." **

The waiter seemed to have some special incite about the feelings of those living in East Berlin. We thanked him and ordered sandwiches and what looked like a Russian version of cola.

"Where do you think the Russians would have brought my dear daughter?" I whispered to Ezekiel.

---

*The Tiergarten is over 520 acres of public gardens in the heart of Berlin. It was originally established in the middle of the sixteenth century as a wild animal game park. In 1742, Fredrick the Great, who disliked hunting, turned the park into a "pleasure park for the people." After being devastated by World War II the park was gradually reforested.

**Access to West Berlin became gradually more restrictive in the early 1950s. After 13 August, 1961, a barrier, known as the Berlin Wall was constructed to prevent East Germans from traveling to West Germany. Many East Germans were shot by East German guards while trying to flee to the western part of Berlin during this period. Before the wall was erected, 3.5 million East Germans circumvented Eastern Block emigration restrictions and fled to the Western sector.

"We should probably start by asking a few general questions of the local police," suggested Ezekiel.

We walked down a fairly wide main street toward the eastern sector of Berlin. We did see a couple of signs stating we were now in East Berlin. We were passing a few shops when we decided to enter a small smoke shop. They sold cigars, pipes, and even some American brands of cigarettes.

"Good afternoon, sir!" Ezekiel's friendly greeting seemed to light up the owner's face.

"I would like to buy a good cigar and perhaps you could give us some directions?"

"Of course, I have some of the best from Havana!"

The shopkeeper proceeded to show us a selection of Cuban cigars which he extracted from a glass case. The cigars were all wrapped in cellophane and the clerk used a tong-like instrument to handle the smokes.

I pointed to two of the cigars and the clerk placed each of them in a small glass vile or tube and sealed the end with a screw top and hot wax.

"This will keep them in top freshness until you are ready to enjoy them."

Since there was no one else in the shop, I quietly asked the shopkeeper if he could direct me to the police station. I told him we were tourists and would like to get some information about getting around the city.

"You are referring to our local police?" The shopkeeper's query was replied in a guarded tone.

"Yes. Also, perhaps the Stasi could be helpful?" I suggested.

All of a sudden, the shopkeeper's face grew dark and foreboding.

"No!" He hissed in a low and threatening voice. "The Stasi are never helpful. Please do not even mention them in this shop again. They have spies everywhere. People who go to their location in the military zone rarely return."

His face had perceptively darkened, his voice was low and his eyes darted around his shop. It was almost as if he had turned into a different person.

"Oh." I spoke with the innocents of a tourist. "Where is this military zone?"

"Please." He whispered in a forceful voice.

"The Stasi have a prison in a restricted military zone which is sealed off from the outside world. It is way down *Landsberger Allee*. No tourists are allowed there. In addition, no one in their right mind would go near that hell-hole!"

We thanked the kind shopkeeper, paid our bill, and headed out into the sunshine.

When outside and away from prying ears, I commented, "Zeke, this might be more difficult than we had first thought."

Ezekiel's immediate response, "Even more difficult than getting out of the *Reich* during the war with a sixteen-year-old teenage girl disguised as your aide?"

"I have to admit, Greta was more of a help than hinderance. I was pleasantly surprised!"

"Let's think while we look for a taxi," whispered Ezekiel in a low voice. "We will need some excellent camouflage and transportation to get into this particular 'hell-hole' of a Stasi prison."

Chapter 22

Procuring Documents

We were walking toward a busier part of East Berlin, looking for a taxi operator when Ezekiel came up with an outline of a plan.

"Jenz, I think the only way to get into the prison, might be similar to the way we were able to get out of the *Reich* during the last few months of the war. We are going to need East German guard uniforms, or some sort of official-looking police or military uniforms.

"It might sound a little dangerous, but I'm pretty sure the prison is not just going to let us go on a tour and visit the inmates!

"It would also be best if we could get some official-looking documents, either Stasi or KGB * identify cards."

"Let's find a hotel room, Zeke. And remember, the rooms could all have listening devices installed, or the phones could all be electronically monitored.

"Once we find a room in a quiet section of Berlin, I will try to get in touch with my old contact that made up your Italian documents when you enrolled in the Technical University in 1937 and then into the *Wehrmacht.*"

---

* KGB was the abbreviation for the Russian secret police. This group of thuggish police officers built the Stasi to their own specifications. They terrorized the citizens of East Germany until Russian President Vladimir Gorbachev instituted the program called Glasnost in 1989. This "transparency" program ended much of the fear of the German population. It was little known at the time, but Gorbachev's grandfather had been in a gulag.

CPSU General Secretary of the Soviet Union, Mikhail Gorbachev instituted a program called Perestroika or political reform that led to the fall of Communism in Eastern Europe and the destruction of the Berlin Wall that encircled the Western Zone of Berlin on the 9th of November 1989.

Once we had found accommodations at a small hotel on Marshall Strasse in the Western Zone, I started making phone calls. I found my contact on the third try, but was careful not to say too much on the phone. Although he had moved twice since I last saw him, his address on Lyndon Strasse wasn't hard to find.

Zeke and I took a cab to within a couple of blocks from his residence and walked to his apartment. Both Zeke and I were careful not to use any names. I introduced Zeke as Vitali Carapezza, the same name from his previous documents.

The document expert said, "Please call me Z.

We told Z that we needed documents to get us into the Stasi Prison in the military zone. At first, he looked at us with an expression of chagrin, but you could tell he was thinking, but then continued after taking a deep breath with a sigh.

"The prison is called Hoenschonhausen. It is for people who oppose the government. Not many people know about its existence, it isn't on any of the city maps. Officially, it doesn't exist! Because it is in the military zone, it is considered impregnable.

"Also, I have heard they are able to torture prisoners by having watertight cells that can be filled with water. The prisoner cannot sit or lie down because the water is waist deep.

"In order to gain access to the prison, you will have to represent high-ranking officials from before the fall of the city to the Russians." Z continued, "You will have to be East Germans or Russians, in full uniforms, with impeccable military documents and complimentary ribbons. It would be helpful if you knew a few Russian words and phrases."

"We can manage all of that," I responded, perhaps too confidently. "How long would you estimate it might take to get the necessary uniforms and documentation?"

"The uniforms can be purchased within a day or two," remarked Z assuredly.

"They will be Russian uniforms representing you both as a Colonel and Lieutenant Colonel in the Russian Army, your insignia will designate you as special branch officers of the KGB. I will make up the necessary documents here; I have the official stamps and paper. Your familiarity with the Russian phrases might take longer.

After I told him why we were there to visit the prison, Z acknowledged, "I will also give you transfer papers and orders from the Kremlin in order to have your daughter transferred to a prison in Russia. These have to look very official from the Vorkuta Prison* in northern Russia.

"Also, I will need to look at your passports in order to procure an East German similar document to place your pictures and proper stamps. The total cost will be approximately two thousand U.S. dollars. Will that be acceptable?"

I paid in cash with U.S. hundred-dollar bills. I mentioned, "These documents have to be convincing for the officials running the Stasi Prison."

Zeke and I left to go to a Russian restaurant to brush up on our East-German and Russian language skills.

The more we learned about the use of the Russian language, the less important it seemed to be able to use it.

---

*Vorkuta Prison was a notoriously harsh prison 110 kilometers above the Arctic Circle in Russia. It was a slave labor camp that produced coal for Russia. The coal was vital for Russian industry during WW II.

Chapter 23

⎯⎯◦◦◦⎯⎯

Our First Test of Russian Documentation

Our "new" uniforms and identification documents looked very authentic. The uniforms were well-worn and looked well-used. Even the military ribbons, indicating many victories against the Nazi forces on the front lines at Kursk, the Vistula, and Berlin, were authentic well-worn indications of our rank, bravery, and importance.

"I gotta tell you, Zeke, these uniforms and ribbons look pretty authentic to me!"

Zeke shot back, "Let's hope the East German guards are duly impressed!"

We decided to test our authenticity at the same restaurant near the Tiergarten where we had lunch when we first arrived in Berlin. Our reception was unusually friendly, but guarded. Most folks in the establishment glanced at us and turned quickly away. Our waiter was courteous, but seemed quite nervous.

"I hope our waiter doesn't get so nervous he drops our food," remarked Zeke.

"It certainly looks like our camouflage is effective," was my retort. "Perhaps we should give our uniforms a try with our helpful smoke-shop friend?"

"I don't know, Jenz. He seemed pretty nervous when he thought we were tourists! I'm not sure what his reaction will be if we walk in dressed in KGB uniforms with all these combat ribbons."

"Let's pay our check-bill and see if he is open today."

When we walked into his shop, it was obvious he didn't recognize us. He was deferential and friendly, but obviously nervous.

"Good afternoon, gentlemen. How can I be of service today?"

"Hello, son." Jenz had taken on a paternal expression. "I will tell you how you can be of service. We purchased two Cuban cigars from you a couple of days ago."

Instant recognition was evident on the poor clerk's face.

"Yes!" He almost shouted. **I hope you found them acceptable. You may certainly have a refund if you found them not to your liking."**

The poor fellow was shaking; sweat was breaking out and beading up on his forehead and upper lip. Fortunately, there were no other customers in the deserted shop.

"I thought you were both tourists. I had no idea you were heroes from the army. You may have whatever you want in this poor shop at no cost to you!"

"We are not looking for handouts, kind sir. We need information."

"Yes, yes. What can I tell you?"

Zeke replied in a friendly tone. "Sir, what can you tell us about the Stasi prison in the military section of East Berlin? We need to visit that institution in order to question a prisoner."

The clerk was very forthcoming with his information. He gave us complete directions and the best time for a visit. He also told us to ask for Lieutenant Shoffner who was his neighbor's son.

"The warden of the prison, his name is Hans Dietrich, is very strict. It would not be too much of stretch to say he is at best, how do I say this, – unstable. If Lieutenant Shoffner could go with you when you meet him, it might help with the warden's unpredictability."

We thanked him for his information and asked if there was anything else he could enlighten us about the prison, since we had never been there.

He squeaked, "Gentlemen, the Stasi prison is a very dangerous place. No one goes there who doesn't have a very good reason. It is a perilous place to visit."

The poor clerk was obviously frightened. He was shaking as we headed for the door.

We left and walked out into the fresh air.

"Well, Zeke. What did you think?"

"I thought our uniforms and decorations seemed to do the trick – at least for our waiter and smoke-shop friend. Perhaps we should wait until first thing tomorrow to test our luck with the prison guards."

"I would love to wait another day, Zeke, but there is no telling what the Russians have planned for my daughter. Let's find a limo service for a ride to the prison.

Chapter 24

The Stasi Prison in East Berlin

It wasn't easy finding a limousine company willing to take us to the Stasi Prison. After two tries, we decided to wear our uniforms and visit an older, established company that had ties to the Hitler administration before the end of the war. The current owner, we discovered after a bit of research, was a friend of Albert Speer, Hitler's architect and Minister of Armaments.

We called ahead to ensure correct directions. We wanted them to be expecting us.

The car service was in a large gray warehouse-looking building with in-and-out driveways. It was in a quiet section of West Berlin, near the airport. The manager's office was within the structure on the second floor.

The manager was expecting us. We hadn't mentioned that we were from the Russian military, so he looked a little surprised and nervous when we entered his second-floor office.

Zeke was very effective in gaining the owner's confidence. Perhaps our uniforms helped a little.

"Sir," Zeke explained, "My Colonel and I have to complete a mission at the local Stasi Prison in the military zone. We are transferring a prisoner to a more secure prison in Russia."

Zeke laid out our orders and paperwork for the owner to look over. We explained to the manager, that we would need the services of one of his best cars and a very reliable and trustworthy driver. In addition, the driver would have to carry a briefcase for us into the prison and wait in the automobile while we interrogated the prisoner before we took the prisoner from the prison in the limousine.

"How long would the driver have to wait for you to exit the prison with the prisoner? asked the manager?

"Is this operation at all dangerous?

Zeke replied, "Sir, we are not exactly sure how long the driver would be waiting for the transfer. It depends a bit on the warden's cooperation. It might take up to two to three hours. I can assure you, however, there would be no danger to your driver or automobile."

"When would you like to engage our services," asked the manager.

"As soon as possible," answered Zeke. "Preferably this afternoon. We do not like to keep unpredictable prisoners in a holding cell too long."

"Let me see who might be available today," replied the manager. He hit an intercom button and asked who was available in the garage for a 3–4-hour trip.

"Hedwig," he spoke into the microphone. "Who is available for a trip this afternoon of possibly up to 4 hours duration?"

"Boss, we have Hermann and Ingrid available right now."

"Ingrid is our most reliable driver, gentlemen."

Chapter 25

Inside the Infamous Stasi Prison

When Greta had been brought into the Stasi Prison for the initial "interview" and indoctrination two things were made very clear to her.

First, she immediately thought, by the guard's leering glances, anyone in that prison would perhaps not treat her well, and possibly use her as a sexual plaything. Second, it would probably be a fight for her life in order to stay alive.

She was forced to wait in a cold, cement block, dimly lit cell for over an hour with some parting harsh words from the guard.

"Girl! Sit here and behave yourself. The warden wants to examine you."

Although those words were not exactly encouraging, Greta knew better than to act defiant. She had no inkling that this cell would be considered a palace compared to what she might face in the future.

"Where am I going to go?" Greta replied in a compliant tone. "My arms are handcuffed to the table and my legs are shackled to the floor!"

"I would advise you to do exactly as the warden requires, girl. He is a very strict man who has needs." The guard spit the words from her mouth as the cell door shut with a loud **clang** behind him.

Greta sat there with her head on her folded arms on the desk. Many thoughts of terror raced through her mind. *She wondered what this warden person was like. Was he reasonable? would he hurt her? Was he a similar despicable man as some of the Gestapo types she had met? Or, was he worse? She wished her father or Jenz and Ezekiel could find her, but all she knew was that she was somewhere in East Berlin.*

There was a rustling at the door as the key turned the latch. In walked what she assumed was the warden and two female assistants. Greta thought, at first, that the assistants were also men, but with closer scrutiny she decided they must be women with very mannish and stern facial expressions.

The warden was a large man with brutish features. His face looked too large for his head because of a balding condition that left only a few wisps of grey hair around his ears. His unshaved face left a stubble that blended into a smooth balding pate. He must have been over six feet tall. His first words were harsh and not at all reassuring.

"Unshackle the prisoner and strip her for a shower and preparation for her prison uniform."

Greta felt the kind of terror that shoots through you with the complete understanding there was absolutely nothing she could do about it.

Both "female" assistant guards grabbed her by the arms, unshackled her hands, and brought her to her feet while tearing off her shirt.

The guards then unshackled her ankles and tore off her pants. Then one of the guards cut off her undergarments with a sharp knife.

Although Greta was terrified, she tried to keep a stoic expression on her face while remembering some of the things Jenz had told her: Never show fear, because then your attackers or tormentors will know they have won and have you under their control; in addition, try to say nothing.

She looked around the cement-block cell, realizing these people thought they now had complete control over her. The warden and two guards in an eight square meter cell standing and looking over her quite appealing and sensuous completely naked seventeen-year-old body.

Greta wanted to shout at them what Jenz would do to these low-life criminals, if he would ever get a hold of them; she said nothing.

The warden, however, seemed to be able to read her thoughts. "Dearie, don't even try to resist us. No one knows where you are. And even if your country would try to get you out of here, no one is allowed into this military zone in East Berlin, unless they have specific business with our institution.

Greta could hold back no longer. **"Be careful you don't touch or harm me, Mr. Warden. My father has a very sensitive disposition, especially when he's hungry!"**

"You don't seem to understand, you pretty young thing," returned the warden in a calm and calculated tone. "No one on the planet can help you now. You are completely under the control of the Stasi system. And, unfortunately for you, **I am the Stasi system!"**

One of the female guards confronted Greta with a low growl. "You better do exactly as Warden Dietrich commands, or you might be placed in a water cell where you would not be able to sit, lie down, or sleep for days at a time."

Greta just stood there and stared at the intimidating guard. Although her thoughts were dark and hateful, she tried not to shake in the cold dank cell. She did not want uncontrollable shaking to darken her outward mood. Her expression was that of grim resignation.

Chapter 26

Gaining Access to the Stasi Prison

Zeke and I wanted to have a friendly business relationship with the driver of the limousine, Ms Ingrid. She was a slightly-built woman, probably forty to fifty years old, who undoubtedly needed this job in order to pay her bills. She seemed a bit nervous.

"Ingrid," Zeke started. "Please do not get intimidated by our uniforms, or the fact that we are going to the infamous Stasi Prison. We have orders from our superiors in Moscow that compel us to go there. We are in the process of transferring a prisoner to an even more secure prison in our homeland.

I added, "Ingrid, if you follow our instructions, nobody will delay us and you will be rewarded for a trip well done. We are transporting a prisoner from the Stasi controlled prison to the Vorkuta Gulag in Siberia. Once we are out of the military section and into the western zone, the prisoner will be transferred to our own personal military vehicle. Do you understand?"

We gave Ms. Ingrid a little more information than she needed in order to gain her confidence that this was an almost routine transfer.

"I think so." Ingrid replied in a somewhat reluctant tone. "Is the prisoner dangerous?"

"Every precaution will be taken," I replied. "The prisoner will be handcuffed and shackled. She is a young female; she will not be resistant; she will pose no threat to you or anyone else."

Although our driver, Ingrid, had to make a stop at a military check-point, our orders and paperwork eventually got us on our way through this military section of East Berlin and on to the Stasi Prison facility.

The prison itself was larger than I anticipated. It resembled a dark, grey warehouse-looking cement structure with all the embellishments of an Albert Speer architectural-style design. I couldn't see an exercise yard for the inmates from where we parked, but there was a looming guard tower on the far corner of the prison.

"Ingrid, please wait in the automobile while the colonel and I retrieve the prisoner," Ezekiel stated in a calm, soothing, almost mellifluent voice.

"How long should this take?" Queried Ingrid.

"Paperwork could take one to three hours, Ingrid.

"However," I stressed, "Please, under no circumstances, leave this car park. It is critical that we are able to have a smooth transfer from this Stasi prison to our homeland facility. The Stasi would not look kindly on any unfortunate slip-ups."

I certainly didn't mean to be intimidating to Ms. Ingrid, but I wanted her to know the importance we placed on this operation. The retrieval of my beloved and precious daughter could be difficult, even dicey and fraught with danger, but we absolutely needed Ingrid not to get nervous, agitated or uneasy. It was essential that she not panic and decide to leave the facility.

Zeke continued, "There will be a nice bonus for you Ms Ingrid, when we complete this mission."

Chapter 27

The Warden's Office

Greta was thrust into the shower. Even though the water gauge indicated "hot" the water was freezing cold. The female guards laughed and tormented her with slurs.

"You weak, skinny little girl; where did you leave your boobs, creampuff? What's the matter? Isn't the water warm enough for you? Sorry, pretty girl; you will never have a warm shower again!"

Greta just stood there with the water hitting her. Her back was toward the guards. After a minute, the frigid water seemed to numb her body to the point she couldn't hear the guards' torments or feel the ice-cold water bouncing off her body. She turned and a smile broke across her face. It was a bit of a grimace, but it was the best she could do. Her teeth shone exceptionally bright and white through her blue lips.

Finally, one of the guards shouted, **"Mine Gott, she almost seems to be enjoying this!"**

The second guard stated in broken German, "Let's get her out of there and dried off. We will let her keep her towel and drag her up to the warden's office. We shall see how much she enjoys the brute's company."

Rough, harsh hands dragged Greta out of the shower and dried off every part of her body with a coarse woolly rag of a towel. The guard's thoroughness and roughness showed no mercy and left her skin red and sore.

Rugged hands pulled Greta along a linoleum corridor and pulled her up a flight of stairs. They stopped in front of an intimidating door marked **Prison Warden.**

The lead guard knocked.

A secretary announced "enter."

Greta was roughly brought into the room. She was greeted by perhaps the ugliest woman she had ever seen. The overweight woman had a bloated, severely pock-marked, very pale face with what looked like traces of a beard and mustache.

The secretary introduced herself by stating in a firm tone, **"My name is Hilda. You will do exactly as I instruct, and you may get to wear one of our prison uniforms without too much bruising on your arms and legs."**

Greta tried to smile, but she was shivering so much her smile was quite forced.

"Oh, you pretty one. You have beautiful teeth!" the secretary hissed. **"You may even get to keep some of them if you follow our rules at this facility."**

Greta tried to conceal a shudder. Hilda seemed to enjoy staring at her body and running her eyes over her breasts.

Hilda was grotesquely corpulent with very thin grey hair streaked across a the beginning of a balding scalp. She had a distinct odor that indicated bathing wasn't a consistent part of her daily routine.

"Place your towel on the chair and sit on it. Do not get the floor wet with your dripping hair. We will have your hair chopped off in the fitting room for your prison uniform after the warden 'inspects' you." Hilda croaked, with all the charm of a rattlesnake.

Greta tried to withdraw into herself but showed no outer sign of her bitter distaste.

Hilda then pressed an intercom button and informed the warden that the prisoner was in her office.

"Send her in alone, Hilda."

Once in the warden's office, Dietrich offered her a small cotton blanket for warmth and to cover her nakedness.

"Greta. You understand you are a prisoner of the Stasi system and there is no escape unless your family complies with my country's wishes?"

"Mistreating me would be a big mistake, Warden Dietrich."

"Unfortunately for you, Ms, your time here in Berlin will not be as long as I had hoped. I have two messages here regarding your status.

"One is from the head of our intelligence service requiring a transfer to another facility immediately.

"And the second is from our front office guard telling me that two officers of the Russian Army are here to escort you to the same facility. It is odd is it not, that both requests arrive within the same hour?"

"I'm cold and hungry. I want my cloths back!"

"My intention was for you to provide me with an afternoon of entertainment, but with these two developments, I will have to postpone our fun-time together."

Warden Dietrich pressed a button on his intercom.

"Hilda, please have the guards remove the prisoner from my office, outfit her with our prison uniform and place her in a holding cell."

A moment later, the two burly female guards came into the warden's office and roughly dragged Greta out to another cell. One of the guards threw in a large grey loose-fitting prison uniform.

Greta thought, *it's not much, but it will cover me up and provide a bit of warmth.* She sat on a wooden bunk with no mattress.

Meanwhile, Warden Dietrich was perplexed.

Why, he thought, would someone arrive at our prison to transfer a prisoner the same hour I have received the message to transfer her. Our communication system isn't that efficient. I need to talk with the Red Army contact for our prison.

"Hilda!" Warden Dietrich called into his intercom. "Get me Colonel Paplovich on the phone. I have a question for him."

After a few minutes the warden's desk phone rang with Colonel Paplovich on the line.

"Warden Dietrich, what can I do for you this afternoon?"

"Sir, I have a special prisoner here in our holding cell. You may realize she is from America. Our country is holding her until we receive word that certain missile technology has been transferred to our country.

"My question is this. Have you sent two Russian Officers here to transfer the prisoner to the Vorkuta Prison?"

"**What!**" Exclaimed the colonel. **"I have ordered no such transfer until next week. Why do you ask such a question?"**

"Because, colonel, there are two Russian Officers here at the prison to take the prisoner to Vorkuta Prison in Russa."

"**Nyet!**" Shouted the Russian colonel. "I will send a special guard with an armored carrier to the prison within the hour to transfer the prisoner. You may let the two officers interview the prisoner, but under no circumstances should this prisoner's transfer be under their control. My hand-picked guards will be at your prison in order to facilitate the transfer."

"**Yes, Sir!**" The warden affirmed.

The warden knew the prisoner transfer was a high priority for his boss, so he instructed Hilda on the intercom, "Hilda, I will personally escort the Russian officers to the prisoner's holding cell."

Chapter 28

⟡

Holding Cell, Stasi Prison

The cell for temporary holding of prisoners was devoid of anything but the bare necessities. Toilet facilities consisted of a bucket in the corner. There were no other toilet niceties. The smell was overpowering. The cement floor looked like it hadn't been swept in months. The walls were grimy cinderblocks. What passed for a bed was a wooden plank covered by a thin blanket. There was no pillow or sheet. There was no light coming into the cell other than the hall lights. There was a hum of machinery in the background and the unmistakable sound of metal slamming against metal as cell doors swung shut.

Greta was comforted in that she could speak and pretty much understand what the guards were saying. She thought to herself, *how could the army be so cruel to its' own citizens? Then she remembered what the Gestapo and the Brown Shirts were all about.*

She also thought about what she might be missing in school. I hope Chasha can catch me up. I'm a long way from Sudbury High School!

Just then she could hear several men coming down the prison corridor. Their boots stomping on the beaten down tile floor. As they came nearer to her cell some voices sounded familiar. It was German with almost an English accent. She backed away from her cell door and plunked herself on the far corner of the hard bed. Although she had been in this prison of horrors only a short time, she quickly learned to dread what could come next.

She looked up and saw Warden Dietrich talking to what looked like two Russian Army Officers. Her heart almost leapt out of her chest when she realized the two Russian Officers were her step-dad Jenz and his lifelong best friend Ezekiel.

She jumped up from her bench but had the presence of mind not to say anything, but she couldn't help herself.

"Warden! I want my cloths back and I need to eat."

"Sit down, prisoner!" Warden Dietrich commanded with authority. These officers have stated that they are taking you to a safe prison in their homeland. I have to go over their paperwork before we can release you from this secure facility.

Then the Warden spoke to the officers. Please come with me while I go over your paperwork.

Jenz, the officer dressed in the Russian Colonel uniform asked with a completely serious face without a hint of humor, "Sir, is the prisoner dangerous?"

"I'm not sure." Warden Dietrich answered. "She has been disrespectful to our guards, but we have not instituted any punitive punishment to this point.

"Please come with me to my office."

As we followed the warden to his office, Zeke glanced at me with an inquiring look on his face. Neither of us could believe our good fortune in being able to free Greta from this abhorrent facility. We had no idea that this facility would look quite grand compared to where we were heading.

As we entered the Warden's office, Hilda, his trusted assistant, gave the warden a message from the guards at the prison reception area.

The message read: *Two Russian guards are in the prison to transfer the prisoner.*

Hilda also mentioned to the warden. "You also had a call from Colonel Popovich. He stated that under no circumstances are you to release the prisoner to anyone but his designated guards."

Zeke and I tried not to let disappointment register on our faces. My immediate reply to the warden, "are you sure this prisoner isn't dangerous?"

The warden looked anxious, "I really have no idea. However, Colonel Paplovich is in control of the Stasi Officers here in the military zone of East Berlin. It would do neither of us any good to go against his wishes."

"We understand completely, Warden Dietrich. Do you have any idea where the prisoner is to be taken in this transfer?"

"It is my understanding," claimed the warden, "That the prisoner is to be immediately transferred to a very secure prison in Vorkuta, Russia. I am not even sure where that particular prison is located, but I believe it is somewhere in Siberia."

Ezekiel and I thanked the warden for his time and mentioned, "I think we can work out something with Colonel Paplovich that will not reflect negatively on your secure prison here in East Berlin."

We made our way back to our waiting automobile without discussing the inconvenience and disappointment we both felt.

Back at our hotel we considered our next step.

Chapter 29

Unpleasant Options

Needless to say, Zeke and I were very disappointed that we couldn't rescue Greta from the clutches of the Stasi Prison system. Although neither of us was despondent, we searched about for answers.

I asked Zeke if he had any suggestions.

"Perhaps Z, our contact for our uniforms and transfer papers, might have some suggestions."

We decided to go back to Z to get his opinion for our missed opportunity.

We called first, and then went over to his apartment.

After we discussed what went on at the Sasi prison, Z said, "Jenz, you and Ezekiel were fortunate to have very authentic looking papers and uniforms. You did not want to get delayed with anyone questioning your papers. You were very smart to make an immediate exit.

"More importantly, I can change the paperwork to indicate a transfer from the Vorkuta Prison to the Butyrka Prison in the Tverskoy District of central Moscow. The paperwork will look very official. I can have them stamped with an embossed stamp indicating top secret from the Kremlin. You could keep the same uniforms without any change in rank or insignia."

Zeke asked, "Just how far is the Vorkuta Prison from Moscow?"

"An excellent question, Sir. My guess is that the prison is at least one thousand kilometers due north of Moscow. It is approximately 160 kilometers (almost 100 miles) north of the Artic Circle in Siberia."

"Do they have a nearby airport?" was my thoughtful question.

"Not only is there no airport, there are no roads!" commented Z.

"The whole area is built on permafrost. It never thaws out in the summer. The prison is only accessible by rail, and even by rail, it is reachable only about seven months of the year.

"As you can surmise, the prison is virtually escape-proof. Even if someone were to make it past the coils of barbed wire, the weather in the winter, and swarms of flying insects and mosquitos in the brief summer, would not permit anyone to get far in their 'white nights.'"

I had never heard of 'white knights.' My immediate question was, "What are the devil are 'white nights?'"

"Oh," said Z. "The sun doesn't set for about 3 months. There are lots of flowers and tons of insects. The midges and mosquitos are deadly. They get in your nose, ears, and eyes. Be prepared if you go up there now in May."

"I will go right away, but I can't speak for you, Ezekiel. This trip could be many times more dangerous than our visit here to the Stasi Prison."

"Jenz, I am with you until we can safely retrieve your precious daughter. I just hope Greta will be as healthy as she appeared this afternoon in the Stasi Prison.

"I would just like to make sure we have everything we need in the way of paper-work and supplies.

"Can you tell us, Z, anything else we should know of the Vorkuta Prison."

"Well," Z spoke hesitantly and with a bit of delay.

"It would be important that you both get to her as soon as she enters the prison. Vorkuta is one of several political prisons. It not only imprisons political dissidents, people opposed to the current regime, and any number of miscreants, but the biggest danger can be from the guards and those who run the gulag system."

"What sort of danger would Greta be facing?" Jenz asked with concerning sincerity.

"Mainly beatings, rape, and murder," replied Z.

"Anyone who doesn't conform to the gulag system right away is beaten or raped by the guards, or fellow prisoners. The trustees, or managers of the prison usually take first pick of the new arrivals and beat or rape them into submission.

"When new admissions are made to the Vorkuta facility, the new inmate is usually roughly shaved, including the head and private areas. This way the guards can completely break down any bit of resistance and let the new arrival know that they are not in control of anything anymore and that they are completely at the mercy of the guards.

"The guards can then judge who are the most sexually desirable for their diabolical wishes. After a week or two, most of the women are continually rapped by the same guard who becomes his or her 'protector.' This 'protector' usually visits at least 2-3 times each week, sometimes more frequently."

"Mine Gott im Himmel, Z. Are what you are telling us accurate?" asked Zeke.

"Unfortunately, gentlemen, I have just touched on the obvious. It would be a very perilous place for any young woman. The guards and trustees are ugly and unstable. They are some of the most brutal men on the planet. Perhaps the system makes them into dreadful atrocious brutes.

"In general, the guards and trustees at the Vorkuta facility are appalling examples of mankind! I wish I could give you both a more positive example of what Greta will be facing if she spends any length of time at Vorkuta."

Ezekiel immediately asked, "Sir, please think hard. Is there anything at all positive you can tell us about the gulag system in general or specifically, Vorkuta?"

Z said, "I'm thinking. In the meantime, can I get anyone a glass of water or something stronger?"

Jenz and I just exchanged glances and declined while Z poured himself about two fingers of a pretty good Schnaps into a whisky glass.

Chapter 30

Learning about Vorkuta Gulag

After downing the liquid refreshment in one gulp, Z made a comment. "There is one thing that may help, but you have to understand one thing about those operating the gulags and those imprisoned."

"Anything would be helpful," Zeke articulated in a measured tone. He then asked an important question that might be hard for Jenz to hear. "Do they subject the prisoners to torture?"

"In general, not usually." Z spoke up right away.

"What you need to know," Z continued, "Is that Vorkuta is a forced labor camp. There is a huge coal mine there that supplies coal to Moscow and eastern Russia. It is an important resource for the population for heating their homes in the winter and driving Russian industry. It was essential during this past war for the Russians to keep this mine operating at maximum efficiency for their war effort.

"Even the women work in the mines."

"What do the Russians use the women for in the mines?" I asked with some trepidation.

"The stronger women," Z explained, "Break up the large hunks of coal that have been blasted out of the coal tunnels and place them in trolleys, the rest of the women pick up the smaller fist-size chunks of coal and carry them out in buckets. It is back-breaking work for both the men and women. But the mine does produce a lot of coal for Mother Russia. Shirkers are regarded as traitors to the state and considered revolutionaries. The slow workers are given punishment details.

"How are the prisoners fed?" Zeke asked an important question.

"There is a mess hall," Z continued, it is a dining area in a separate hut. The meals are usually a thin soup[*] made with often spoiled cabbages and potatoes with occasional pig-fat in the vat. The meal is usually accompanied with a dark, sometimes moldy bread.

There are no breaks except for the noon meal. You will not find anyone overweight in a Russian gulag. Food is used as a bonus for those who do not cause trouble, are excellent workers, or for those who submit for sexual favors. [**]

I asked, "Is there any health care for those injured or sick?"

Z had a reluctant comment. "Yes. They do have doctors and nurses on their staff at the hospital. They are committed to keeping the slave laborers working as hard as possible for as long as possible. In the winter, conditions can become completely dire."

"What do you mean by dire?" Zeke quickly asked.

"There is very little sunlight after October. The sun sets, and doesn't return until the middle of March. The winter storms are driven by a viscous wind. The prisoners call it the howling darkness. Occasionally the snow gets so deep, the prisoners cannot leave their huts. There is only a sheet metal stove in the huts and as many as 40-70 men or women per hut. The total prison population of Vorkuta is over 60,000 prisoners.

"If the snow continues to fall without let-up in the long fridged months, and the inmates run out of coal, they have to break up

---

* Prison soup was called *balanda* in Russian. It provided, along with a hard, dark bread, sustenance for millions of slave-workers during the Gulag period.

** Withholding food was frequently used as punishment. Complete isolation in a punishment cell was kept for the most difficult prisoners. In Vorkuta the outside punishment cells in the winter meant certain death from freezing.

Most punishments were not specifically to make prisoners suffer. It would be most accurate to say that no one cared if they suffered or not. The important goal at the gulags was weekly production. At Vorkuta it was weekly production of coal. Not much else mattered to any of the camp's administrators.

whatever flimsy furniture they posses in their huts and burn it in their stoves. The snow often completely covers the huts, but does offer a degree of insulation.

"You should understand that those who find themselves in the gulag system are usually the poorest of the poor. Not only are they, for the most part uneducated, impoverished and destitute, but they are the down-and-out members of a very poverty-stricken population. Of course, there are also political dissenters and some intellectuals.

"I will give you an example.

"If a Russian soldier came across a dead German Wehrmacht officer or enlisted man during the war, stealing the deceased soldier's watch would represent more wealth than the soldier would have ever amassed in his life."

"How does this help us?"

I asked.

"What I am suggesting," Z commented, "Vorkuta guards, trustees, and inmates, are very open and subject to bribing."

"We have to pay in order to interact with the prisoners, even with our Russian uniforms and transfer papers?" Zeke asked in a quiet voice.

Z shot back, "I'm just suggesting it might be quite helpful, depending on the circumstances."

"What are the standard bribes for these miscreants?" Zeke asked with sincerity.

"You have to be careful here." Stated Z.

"If you offer too much money, they will get immediately suspicious and it might not go well for you. I would start with a small amount. However, the type of money is also important. You will need some Rubles, Dollars, Pounds and coins. The larger the coin, the better. Many Russians are skeptical of paper money, especially the Ruble.

"Silver coins are always in demand. If you can find some silver U.S. dollars or silver ½ dollars, they would be quite effective in getting you in and out of some difficult places.

Chapter 31

Greta's Difficult Journey

Greta sat in her Stasi holding cell for over an hour waiting for Jenz and Ezekiel to return. She was excited after seeing her loved ones. She did wonder how they had gotten through all the East Berlin security. She was happy and smiling when two Russian guards and the warden came down into her cell-block and stood outside her barred door.

"Prisoner!" Shouted the warden

Greta jumped up off her bed. She couldn't believe her dad and Ezekiel had gotten to her so soon after she was incarcerated in the Stasi Prison. She wondered if they had needed to bribe some official or had just beat one of them into submission.

"Stand at the far corner of the cell!" The warden sounded pretty serious. He probably wasn't thrilled about being outmaneuvered by her father.

"Stand still while the guards place you in shackles!

The warden sounded pretty heated; Greta wondered what her father and Zeke had done to get her released so quickly.

The guards entered her cell and immediately placed handcuffs joined by a short chain on her wrists and the same on her ankles. The guards, both of whom seemed like beefy, ugly, monsters, dragged her out of her cell and to a waiting black older Mercedes automobile. Her handcuffs were attached to a locked chain across the back seat.

Greta was in a terrific mood, knowing she was on her way home to Sudbury.

When they arrived at the Schönefeld Airport, Greta was amazed at how quickly they moved through customs. It seemed even more amazing when they went around all the passengers boarding the aircraft and took a seat in the first row of the plane.

Although her shackles were quite prominent, most of the other passengers didn't seem to pay any attention to them. Her suspicions were tweaked when she noticed most of the passengers were speaking Polish or Russian.

She asked the flight attendant. "Ms, where is this plane headed?"

The flight attendant spoke up in clear and concise voice in fluent German. "Our first stop is Krakow, Poland. Our next leg is flight-planned for the six-hour flight to Moscow."

Greta was stunned. How could her father arrange for this flight to go east toward Poland and then to Moscow in the heart of Eastern Russia?

When she asked the guards where they were headed, they gave her short, gruff answers, but told her they were certainly not going where she was going.

This was confusing to Greta, so she asked, "Where am I going to wind up for my final destination?"

The first guard looked at the other guard and said, "We might as well tell her, Boris."

Boris spoke with a bit of a smirk on his face. "Little girl, you are going to our famous prison in Siberia. Vorkuta Gulag has never had a successful escape. It is located approximately fifteen hundred miles north of Moscow in one of the cruelest and most difficult part of our country. It is one of our hardest and most dangerous of all our gulags. You will never be heard from again!"

A shudder went through Greta. She felt helpless. How would Jenz and Ezekiel ever track her in this remote place? She immediately sunk into a deep depression and fell into an agitated and troubled sleep.

Greta's next conscious thought came as the plane came in for a bouncing landing at the airport in Moscow. There were some exclamations from a few of the passengers, but no one seemed to think the landing was anything but usual.

Greta was dragged off the plane after all the other passengers had de-planed. There were two other guards in a waiting automobile. Papers and a brief exchange of words accompanied her as she was thrust into the back seat.

From what she could understand, these new guards were going to take her to a train station and accompany her to the new prison north of Moscow.

Greta slept most of the time on the train after eating some stale dark bread and some thin potato-vegetable soup. She wondered if any of the other passengers on the train had anything more palatable to eat. What surprised her most was the length of the train ride.

During the lengthy train journey, Greta could hear her guards arguing.

The largest and most brutish guard stated, "I would like to get a taste of the new prisoner before we let the prison guards at Vorkuta continuously rape her."

"I wouldn't blame you," replied the older, and wiser, second guard. "However, according to the transfer papers going along with the prisoner, she is to be delivered 'in a healthy state.' We do not want to take the chance of going against the hierarchy in Moscow and also winding up in that terrible place.

"There are plenty of other women prisoners in the back who wouldn't dare complain about whatever you want to do to them!"

After two stops in Moscow, the landscape was desolate. They passed through forests, valleys and completely unpopulated areas without seeing a sole. The train finally arrived in Vorkuta on the morning of the third day. Greta was met by the most inhospitable guards imaginable.

Two women dragged her off the train. Greta noticed that although they were large women, both of them seemed gaunt with sunken-in faces and no teeth. They both spoke to her with minimal shouts of abusive verbal commands.

The two guards brought Greta to a building that looked like a low Quonset hut. Although it was early in May with a very bright-blue sky, it was cool, probably just above freezing. She shivered in her thin Stasi prison uniform.

The guards roughly sat Greta down and proceeded to cut off her hair.

"Why are you cutting off all my hair?" Greta shouted, appalled.

"Quiet!" Shouted the tallest Russian guard.

A strong facial **Slap** was issued by the second guard. It knocked Greta off her chair and sent her sprawling onto the dirt floor; the slap caused a large red welt on the side of her face.

The second guard shouted at her. **"Bitch, you have a pretty smile today, keep it while you can. In a year or two, you will have lost most of your teeth and your face will cave in, just like ours!"**

The first guard roughly tore off Greta's clothes and thrust her into a cold shower. After a brief wet-down, both guards pulled Greta into her original chair and shaved her head and private parts. She was shivering so hard; it was hard for the guard to shave her properly.

Greta protested and fought back, but to no avail; she stopped struggling and complaining when the largest guard started to wind up for another slap. The first guard said she was lucky because one of the male guards or trustees usually do the shaving so they can choose their 'prison wife' early in the woman's incarceration. Don't worry pretty one, the men usually wait until night-time before they come into the women's hut for their sexual gratification.

"If you don't protest too much," the second guard suggested, "It should go easier for you. If you protest or fight, these guards and trustees can be brutal, and you will never protest again."

Greta gave a shudder as the second guard tossed a dirty towel and prison garb at her and shouted. **"Get dressed quickly and follow me to your new home for the next ten years.**

That night, Greta hid under her bed, but she could hear the brutal sounds and cries of women being raped and beaten. Protesting the rough treatment was useless. No one came to help these poor beaten-down women.

As a new prisoner to the hut her bunk was closest to the *parasha,* or slop bucket. The smell was overpowering. Her sleep on the dirt floor was fitful.

After a breakfast of watery-thin potato soup, Greta was instructed on the work detail where she would participate.

"You look young and healthy!" One of the guards established in a loud, gruff tone. "Your job will be down in the mine." After a 30-minute walk in unison with the other prisoners, he showed her the elevator and gave her a shovel and bucket.

"See that the bucket is completely full before emptying it in the trolly. **It would be unhealthy for you to be a shirker and considered an enemy of the state."**

Greta thought, *it looks unhealthy to even be in the mine. The elevator looks extremely rickety and far from safe.*

But she kept her thoughts to herself. It probably would do no good to protest, in addition, she had some trouble remembering the smattering of Russian language she did understand. She also wanted to avoid any further bruising to her aching body.

Greta was tired and completely exhausted at the end of her ten-hour shift. Her only break was the sparce noon- time meal of thin soup and dark bread. She found it difficult not being able to talk with any of the other women, even though she felt some of them must speak German.

After the evening meal, Greta, completely beaten down, crawled onto her bunk. She wondered what all the commotion was at the front of the hut, when two of the male trustees barged in and screamed at the women as the overhead lights were snaped on: **"Attention at your bunks, ladies, stand for inspection!"**

Chapter 32

Day One at Vorkuta

The official-looking papers for prisoner transfer from the Vorkuta Prison to the Butyrka Prison in the Tverskoy District of Central Moscow were ready for Jenz and Ezekiel the next day.

By waiting until 1 pm they were able to get a direct flight from East Berlin's Schönefeld Airport to Moscow's Sheremetyevo Airdrome. Since they were in uniform and had orders, the flight cost them nothing.

On the train service to Vorkuta Gulag, the journey didn't cost anything, but they had to pay for their food.

Zeke's comment during their first meal on the train, in a low tone, almost a whisper, "I wouldn't feed this to animals!"

"Let's see if we can get some fresh bread or soft drink." Agreed Jenz.

All they were serving on the train was water or vodka. The bread, however, was dark, chewy and not too bad. The water was anyone's guess but was bottled from a large "cooler."

Most of their fellow passengers gave them a wide berth with very little eye contact. Because of their uniforms, no one would have eye contact or speak to them, even when they purchased food. Fear and intimidation were all too evident.

There were no sleeping facilities, but some of the wooden seats would tip back for occasional sleeping. Although the sleeping position was uncomfortable the constant click-clack of the train helped the officers glean a modicum of sleep.

The passageways on the train looked like they hadn't been swept in years. They almost looked like dirt floors covered with sawdust.

The bath facilities were quite rudimentary. The one holer in the rear of each car sent the waste directly onto the railroad tracks; the smell was atrocious. There was a slop bucket in the corner for use when the train was within the city limits. There were no facilities for washing or shaving.

The two officers were riding in the most luxurious part of the train. The first two train cars carried a very few passengers. The rest of the eight train cars were made up of prisoner carriages. These consisted of wooden benches and slop buckets; they were packed with dispirited soles.

Who knows if these poor mortals packed into the overcrowded prison coaches were actual criminals, political dissidents, or just folks unlucky enough to get swept into the gulag system by nosey neighbors, or discarded by disgruntled lovers.

The train made three stops in Moscow the first day. The first 1-hour stop was at Lubyanka Prison.* This building seemed to house the guards for the prisoners which were loaded at the next two stops at Butyrka Prison and Lefortovo Prison.

Those prisoners who were hoarded and whipped on to the prison carriages at Butyrka Prison seemed to be better dressed and were probably mostly political prisoners or intellectuals.

Jenz and Ezekiel gratefully disembarked in the small town of Vorkuta at the end of the third day. They engaged a driver directly at the station. Open trucks were there to transport the prisoners directly to the prison.

With the flash of a silver U.S. fifty-cent coin, they convinced the driver to pull his horse-drawn buggy-wagon directly to the prison. The driver, however, ardently refused to go into the prison.

---

*The Lubyanka Building has ceased to be a prison today. The cells have been turned into offices and storage. The American U-2 pilot, Gary Powers, whose spy plane was shot down in 1960 over Soviet territory, was the last person incarcerated in its cells. (From *"Gulag – A History,"* by Anne Applebaum, Anchor Books, Random House Inc., New York, 2003).

"Nyet! Nyet!"

The buggy driver waved his arms and his reaction was quite vociferous, until another fifty-cent coin was produced and offered. The driver then reluctantly entered the guard tower gate and asked directions to the warden's office.

Ezekiel asked in broken Russian, "Guard, what does the writing mean on the gate over the entrance?"

"Very simple," the guard replied: **Work in the USSR is a matter of Honor and Glory.**

"Mine Gott," uttered Zeke. "Could this place be as bad as Auschwitz?"

The warden carefully examined the embossed orders from the central command in Moscow. Although skeptical, he continually ran his fingers over the embossed seal of the NKVD. * In all likelihood, the warden either couldn't read or understand what was in the transfer papers.

He read the name of the prisoner, Greta Ramsgrund, and muttered, "Is she German or Polish?"

Ezekiel answered in pretty decent Russian. "We believe the prisoner is Swedish. However, she must be shackled before we take her into custody for the trip to the Burtynsky Prison in Moscow. We were not informed if she was dangerous."

The warden pondered the orders with careful consideration, not because he didn't believe them, but he hadn't had a strange request like this in the past. He kept running his fingers over the embossed NKVD seal. That seal put a hard fear into the heart of every Russian.

---

* NKVD stands for The Peoples Commissariat for Internal Affairs. Its main purpose was to protect the state security through political repression; this included authorized murders, kidnappings, assassinations, and mass deportations to one of the over 400 Gulags throughout the Soviet Union.

The NKVD was first established in October 1917. Although this organization is universally hated by citizens of the Soviet Union, it has had several abbreviated names including Cheka – GPU – OGPU – NKGB – NKVD – and - KGB. All of these organizations were known as the secret police.

He finally acknowledged the two officers. "Sirs, there is nothing I can do this late in the evening. I will have a trustee take you to the prisoner barracks directly after the morning meal which is at 0600.

"Please find lodgings this evening at the local Tsentralnaya Hotel. Officers with orders will have a reduced rate. I don't recommend the Vorkuta Hotel; it has too many problems with insects and rodents. I will have my driver take you to the hotel."

"Thank you," Jenz offered, then asked. "Is the prisoner safely incarcerated in her cell?"

"Gentlemen," the warden replied. "There are no cells here in Vorkuta. There is no escape from our very secure facility here at the Vorkuta Gulag.

"How is that?" Ezekiel asked.

"There is nowhere to escape to! The prisoners are housed in barracks.

"The prison has no walls. Only barbed wire rolls and fencing surround the camp. Every Sunday the prisoners are free to walk around the camp, although in the winter, it is totally dark and not practical - indeed it can be deadly - with the howling wind and snow. Some prisoners can even go into the town for shopping on Sunday if the weather isn't too extreme.

Chapter 33

The Horror of Vorkuta

Jenz and Ezekiel had a fitful sleep at the Tsentralnaya Hotel, but at least they were able to shower with a little almost-warm water. Both men were worried how Greta was faring.

Two of the male trustees had burst into the Greta's hut that evening. Even though it was full daylight outside, no windows in the barrack made it dark inside. The trustee switched on the bright overhead lights, and ordered the women: **"Stand for inspection!"** *

All the women immediately came to attention at the foot of their bunks. The two trustees each grabbed a short length of rubber hose clipped to the wall at the entrance of the hut. The first prisoner they came to was bracing the back of her legs against the foot of her bunk.

"Stand straight with no leaning!" Barked the trustee. **"Don't you understand orders?"** **Smack!** The rubber hose snapped across the poor woman's back. She was rewarded with a large red welt that started to bleed through her thin nightshirt.

"You women must follow all the rules of the camp. Anyone caught in the *zapretnaya sona,* (forbidden zone) will be shot by our guards.

"If you have questions or any troubles whatsoever, bring it to the *starista* (prisoner functionary or mediator) in your barracks.

---

*Surprise inspections were part of the climate of fear and intimidation fostered by the Gulag system. This intimidation and cruelty spread to every Soviet citizen in Russia. The climate of generalized anxiety and dread diminished somewhat after Stalin's death in March 1953.

"The morning routine, as you know, begins at 0600. After your morning meal, the *rasvod* (organizing the prisoners into brigades to march to their work detail) will be sounded by a whistle. Do not step out of line, to the right or left, or you could be shot as an escapee."

As the trustee went to shut off the bright overhead lights, he smirked as his last comment was ominous. **"Don't let the guards keep you ladies up too late tonight!"**

Greta asked the woman in the next bunk in broken Russian. "What does that last comment mean?"

"Oh, dearie! You should know that if you haven't had a visit from a regular guard, it could be open season on you. A guard has not chosen you as a prison wife, yet. But the remark by the trustee means they are coming again tonight."

"Is there any way to fight them off?" Greta asked with not a lot of hope in her bunk-mates answer.

"Fighting or complaining would be very foolish," replied the woman in the next bunk.

"A few weeks ago," the woman continued. "One of the new prisoners tried to fight off the brutish guard. She received a broken jaw and lost a good many teeth for her efforts. In addition, she was so bruised and battered it took a week in the prison hospital to have her recover enough to go back to work in the coal mine.

"She has never complained again, and her jaw never did heal properly. She doesn't sound right when she tries to speak, and she has difficulty eating anything solid."

Greta, shivering in fear, grabbed her thin blanket around her and crawled under her bunk. Exhausted from working in the coal mine all day, she finally fell into a deep and troubled sleep.

She slept so soundly, she didn't hear the morning bell at 0600 and missed the morning *rasvod*.

Since the count was off, the march to work in the mines was delayed. A brutish guard came into the barrack yelling for the missing prisoner.

The raucous yelling awakened Greta, but she didn't dare to move. The next thing she felt was strong rough hands grasping her ankles and ripping her out from under her bunk.

The guard barked, **"Get on your bed, sweetie! You are my property this morning."** He went to the entrance and shouted to the *rasvod*. **Move on to the mines; I will be delayed.**

The brutish guard then turned to Greta and commanded, **"Do not rcsist, girlie, or it will not go well for you!"**

The guard tore Greta's cloths off and climbed on top of her.

Greta clenched her jaw, tensed her body and said nothing. She tried to direct her thoughts back to her life in Sudbury as a high-school student with her friend Chasha. However, her thoughts kept drifting back to her frightening experience in her native Germany at her home as the Gestapo attempted to rape her in front of her father.

As the barbarous guard was brutally raping Greta, his vicious comment was merciless. **"You will be my prison wife, dearie. Do not resist! I do not want to scar your pretty face."**

Chapter 34

The Arduous and Painful Routine

It was the second day of her incarceration when one of the women from her hut spoke to Greta in fluent and obviously well-educated German at the noontime meal.

"Your name is Greta, is it not?

"Yes, how would you know my name?"

"I have heard you complain in German."

"Miss, you will get use to the routine here at Vorkuta after a few months. Please store up your courage and energy while the sun is shining. The winters here in Siberia can be more depressing than you could ever imagine. If you are not prepared for them, the cold and the howling wind can crush your spirit."

"My God," declared Greta. "Can this place get worse than being continuously raped by the guards and sleeping in bug-infested huts?"

"Look, Greta. You haven't been badly beaten yet. Believe me, things can get much worse.

"Oh, please don't say that!" Greta replied. "What is your name and why are you here?"

"My name is Sasha. I have been one of the *zeks* (prisoners) here in this *lagpunkt* (prison) after being arrested two years ago. I was a student at the university in Leningrad and was detained by the NKVD for participating in a student protest against poor food at the school.

"You are lucky that it has been only one guard that has attacked you. I thought I was going to be killed by a few of the bestial guards that raped me.

"I tried to complain to one of the camp trustees, but he came in and raped me that very night. He told me I was lucky to be alive and that I'd better not ever complain again."

"Oh, Sasha! That sounds terrible. How did you survive that first winter with a different guard raping you almost each night?"

"I should have learned sooner not to fight these demons. When I was first brought here, I had beautiful long blond hair. I resisted when they began to cut it all off and began shaving my head. Not only did they give me a nasty cut on my head, but they also cut me when they were shaving my genitals. It was very painful for weeks and took forever to heal. I thought the continuous rapes would kill me.

"If you conform to the routine, it will go better for you, Greta. Try not to feel the brutality of the rapes. In my mind, I put myself in a different place during each ordeal. I clench my teeth and think of my childhood growing up with my loving parents in a quiet and lovely part of Berlin.

"We lived on Tiegartens Strasse. The park was our front yard."

"It sounds beautiful, Sasha.

"Once, my stepfather, Jenz, told me about a time when he rescued my stepmother, Ilse, from a monster Gestapo Agent near that park. He was about to rape her and enslave her.

"What was the charge for you being arrested?" Greta asked.

"It was quite non-specific. Breaking the peace and disturbing the school day were given. My boyfriend then tried to intervene and claimed the charges were weak and pathetic.

"The authorities, the NKVD, took us out to the back of the school cafeteria where all the students could see us. One of the secret police agents then pulled out a pistol and shot my boyfriend in the head in front of me and in full view of the rest of the students who were eating their lunch. His blood splashed all over me! I thought I was going to die."

"Sasha, didn't the police come and arrest the killer?"

"You don't understand, Greta. The police were the ones who shot and killed my boyfriend; shot him in the head!"

"Did you get a court hearing by a judge?"

"No, Greta. That is not how it is done here in Russia. All the protesters were brought to the police station where a magistrate told us of our sentence. The ten years in a gulag was supposed to 'reform our thinking and make us better workers for Mother Russia.' The entire court experience was a sham."

"The authorities forced us into railroad cars filled with straw on the wooden floorboards. They took all the protestors and several hundred other unfortunates to the gulags throughout Russia. My misfortune was to wind up here at Vorkuta."

"Many of the newly arrested prisoners were students, political protesters, newspeople, and even military officers who complained about the way their ordinary troops were being treated. *

"How long is your sentence, Greta?"

"I have no idea. I was kidnapped from my high school in America, drugged, and brought to a Stasi prison in East Berlin. I briefly thought I was being rescued by my father and his friend when I learned the Russian Police were transferring me to this horrible and appalling place."

---

*Recent news stories demonstrate the political situation in Russia has not changed too much since Greta's incarceration. 17 May 2024, Reuters News Service reported that Major General Ivan Popov, Commander of Russia's 58th Army in the Ukraine was dismissed from his post and arrested for "fraud and criticism of President Putin's lack of support for his troops."

Early in 2023, the Leader of the Wagner Group, Yevgeny Prigozhin, criticized Putin for lack of support for his front-line troops and attempted a coup. He was killed in a suspicious airplane crash later that year on 24 August 2023.

"Did they not give you an idea of how long you were to be incarcerated here?"

"Never! The guards just told me I was going to a place where no one would ever find me."

133

"Did they not give you an idea of how long you were to be incarcerated here?"

"Never! The guards just told me I was going to a place where no one would ever find me."

Chapter 35

The Arrest

"Sasha, can I ask you a question? There is one thing I haven't been able to understand."

"I will do my best, Greta. What is it you would like to know."

"I understand there are over sixty-thousand prisoners in this camp. Are there other camps this big?"

"Some are larger. There are over 400 of these gulags in the system." Sasha affirmed.

"How is it possible to arrest so many people to keep these prisons full? Are all of them slave-labor camps?"

"The government of Russia, with Stalin as a brutal dictator, has decided that the camps are an excellent way to get rid of anyone who might disagree with his communist philosophy.

"In addition, all the slave labor goes to help keep the government running and gives the economy a competitive edge.

"However, the real plus for the government is the intimidation factor."

Greta asked, "What is the intimidation factor?"

"Look at this way, Greta. How many of the students at my university in Leningrad do you think would now even consider protesting about anything?"

"Oh, Sasha. There must be some way out of this nightmare of a prison."

"The other prisoners tell me the only way to escape is to die. Most of the other women here tell me going along with the camp routine is the least painful way of living. Besides, if you die, the camp officials can't bury you because the ground is frozen just beneath the surface."

"If my father could ever get to this place, I am sure he could save me."

"Greta, that is a fantasy. We are so far from civilization, that no one ever comes here except prisoners by cattle car.

"I do think you should keep that hope of escape or rescue alive. Even though my hope for returning to my native Berlin and my family are all but buried, I shouldn't discourage you."

"What were you studying at the university?" Greta asked.

"I wanted to eventually study the law and perhaps go into politics. I felt women hadn't been heard enough in world affairs, and I admired strong women like Golda Meir, * Indira Ghandhi, ** and Queen Elizabeth, *** along with so many others.

"I recognized, that if given a voice, I could make a difference in so many people's lives, even the health and spirit of our fellow prisoners. I have come to realize; however, I will never get out of this frigid prison. So, my dreams will never come to reality."

"What if I told you in confidence, I still have a hope of being rescued from this desolate place?"

"Greta, I would tell you to hold on to that dream – but it is, unfortunately only a dream."

"Sasha," Greta asked. "If my father could find me here, would you like to go back home to your family in Berlin?"

---

*Golda Meir was the Labor Minister of Israel in the early 1950s. She later became the Israeli Prime Minister and served from 17 March 1969 to 3 June 1974.

**Indira Gandhi was a rising star in India in the early 1950s.

*** Queen Elisabeth ll served her country during WW II as an ambulance driver and Figurehead of the British Commonwealth of Nations from 6 February 1952 to her death in September 2022

"What a question, dear Greta. I would give anything to see my parents and friends again. They probably think I have been killed by now. I have tried to send them letters, but the guards tell me they may never get delivered. I have never received a letter from any of my relatives or friends.

"I don't even know if they know where I am. I do know they could never possibly get here."

"My father and Ezekiel will probably have difficulty finding me, but they developed some very special skills during the war that may be of some help for them."

"What skills are you talking about, Greta?"

"Well, during the war these two men were able to take down several members of the Gestapo. Also, they were involved in secret work in northern Germany during the war. They tried to hinder the development of Nazi missile weapons.

"In addition, they were able to get me out of Nazi Germany and into Sweden. After the war, I came with Jenz and his wife, Ilsa, to America. I was a third-year high school student in a small town outside of Boston, Massachusetts when the Russians took me.

"When I saw my father and Ezekiel in the Stasi prison, I almost didn't recognize them because they had on Russian Officer uniforms."

"Do you really think they will find you in this completely remote area?" Sasha asked. "The Stasi prison in East Berlin is much more easily located than this obscure and inaccessible hell we are living in now. Besides, no one has probably ever heard of this place!"

"If anyone on earth could find me, it would be Jenz and Ezekiel. If they ever show up here, I will ask if they could take you back to Berlin."

"Oh, Greta! Don't give me any hope. I know I am stuck here – probably I will die here. But thank you for your encouraging words."

"We both need encouragement. The coal mine is such a dangerous place to work. Where are you working, Sasha?"

"Most of the first year I was working in the mine, but I got hurt when a trolly ran over my leg and broke it. Since I couldn't work very well in the mines, the administration put me in the kitchen cooking and cleaning. It turned out to be a blessing. The kitchen was the only place where I could get warm in this whole camp this past winter."

"If Ezekiel and my father ever find this place, I will ask them if you could escape with us."

Chapter 36

Jenz and Esekiel Arrive at Greta's Hut

The emaciated-looking trustee from the warden's office walked Jenz and Ezekiel over to the hut where the new prisoner was living.

The guard left them with a short verbal message. "If the prisoner is not in the hut, come back to the warden's office and I will direct you to the mine entrance where she is to be assigned today."

"Thanks!" Zeke said. "We appreciate your help. I'm sure we can find this prisoner."

As they entered the almost totally dark hut, whimpering noises could be heard down at the far end.

The savage guard on top of Greta was so involved in his barbarous work, he didn't hear the two men enter the hut. He did, however, sense that someone had come in. He could see the light flooding into the hut as the main door opened and closed.

Greta was praying for her dad to rescue her. Her eyes were tightly shut. Her body tense and shaking.

Worse for the guard, he thought he caught a glimpse of an officer's hat in the shadow that came through the door.

The brute immediately covered Greta's mouth and told her, "Do not utter a sound, or it will be the end of you. Get your belongings and shoes on and we are leaving by the back entrance. I will bring you to your workplace in the mine."

As Jenz and Ezekiel walked toward the back of the hut, they could see a flash of light from the rear entrance as the door closed after two figures disappeared into the sunlight.

Ezekiel asked, "Who do you think just left the barracks?"

"I'm… I'm not sure, Zeke." It didn't look like Greta, unless she recently cut off all of her hair. One of those people was completely bald."

"I think the prisoners are all shaved of their hair when they enter this hall of horrors, Jenz. Let's quietly follow them to wherever they are going. It looked like one of the guards was dragging someone out."

After following the two figures between the buildings for almost twenty minutes they caught a sight of two people entering a large open area with a continuous flow of small carts hauling coal from the mine. The bedraggled prisoners pushing and pulling wheel-barrel carts of coal out of the mine were too occupied to notice anyone. Otherwise, there was no one around.

Ezekiel commented in a quiet tone. "That could be Greta."

There was a shed-like building to the right of what looked like a crude elevator shaft. The two figures got into the elevator and immediately started descending.

Jenz talked quietly to Ezekiel. "It looks like they have descended into the mine. Let's get into that nearby shed so no one will notice our uniforms.

The shed was a crudely-built but sturdy structure that had lockers and a stove for warming in the cruel long winter months in Siberia. It was evidently a place for the guards to get out of the wind while directing the workers into the mine. Fortunately, it was completely empty in the short summer months.

"Look, Zeke; I am going to remove my uniform jacket and hat and put on one of these work aprons. If Greta is on a work-detail in the mine, I will find her and get her out. I certainly don't expect you to go with me. This could be extremely dangerous."

"Please, Jenz. I have no intension of letting you go into that hell-hole of a mine alone. There is no telling what you may encounter down there. Let's store our uniforms here and grab some coveralls, aprons and crude head scarfs and get down there as soon as possible."

As the two men from Massachusetts descended into the mine on the rather eerie and scary shaking elevator, Jenz commented, "I'm not sure this contraption would pass even Russian standards for a safe elevator."

As both men hung on to the sides of the jouncing box structure, Ezekiel whispered, "Let's use guttural German or sign language to communicate when we reach the level where work is being accomplished. We don't want questions raised about our language."

They kept descending for what seemed like forever into the dark. As they neared the mine floor, the light from distant headlamp lights crept into the shaft.

The crude elevator came to a jarring halt amid a cloud of coal dust and the noise of distant clanging of pick-axes. There was a continuous rumble of coal being broken and tossed into carts.

There must have been hundreds of men and women working off the main tunnel that sloped gradually even deeper into the abyss.

"Jenz," mouthed Ezekiel. "How are we supposed to find anyone in this maze of dark tunnels and coal dust? Nobody here speaks English or understands German. My limited Russian may be more dangerous than helpful."

"I think we can use these limitations to our advantage, Ezekiel. The Russian slang word for prisoner is *zek*. If we call out in each tunnel or to each group of prisoners for '*zek* Greta,' it may be slang, but only one prisoner will understand what we saying."

"It may work, Jenz. We should cover-up our boots with coal dust in order to complete our camouflage.

Chapter 37

Deep in the Vorkuta Coal Mine

After looking and searching for over an hour, Zeke spoke up. "Jenz. I know we have been in even more dangerous places: Auschwitz, Treblinka, Sorbibor, to name a few; and our encounters with the Gestapo come to mind. However, this place gives me the creeps. It gives me the feeling of being buried alive."

Boom! A distant underground explosion rattled the ceiling timbers and shook the ground. Dust descended from the ceiling and rose up from the floor. The walls shook with temerity from the underground waves and reverberations of the explosion. The secondary rumblings were even more unnerving.

The timbers bracing the walls proved little solace for the two men unfamiliar with working in coal mines. Jenz braced himself on one of the supporting logs holding up the ceiling.

Ezekiel mentioned, "I'm not sure hanging on to the bracing timbers is the best idea, Jenz.

"The explosion could have been dynamite going off deep in a coal seam to break away the seam from the walls."

Just then there was a deep throated crashing rumble from deep in the mine. One of the side tunnels several hundred meters down the slopping main tunnel coughed out clouds of dust and debris signaling the complete collapse of the tunnel.

Dust-covered mine workers started streaming out of the tunnels and heading for the main tunnel entrance. Even though the main tunnel exit was over a mile through a dimly-lighted and tenuously-braced tunnel, the uphill sloping rock-strewn climb was worth it. No one trusted the rickety elevator during a mine emergency.

Emergency horns were blaring all over the mine. On the surface, all coal removal operations were halted.

The mine supervisor was deeply worried. He wasn't at all concerned with the loss of prisoner's lives, he had a steady supply of prison labor workers, no matter what their crime had been. However, the emergency would slow down his production tonnage which had to be reported weekly to his superiors in Moscow.

Jenz and Ezekiel had a hushed conversation over the clamor of escaping minors leaving for fresh air.

Jenz shouted, **"Zeke, let's try and cry out to the passing hoard of workers heading for safety."**

Both men repeatedly called out, **"*zek,* Greta, zek Greta,"** as the hundreds of emaciated prisoners rushed by on their way to safety. To the minors, it only sounded like gibberish.

The stampede of prisoners was followed by an earie quiet. Even the emergency horns had stopped blaring.

Jenz and Ezekiel started slowly walking down the main tunnel and calling out in the side tunnels for Greta.

As they edged closer to the tunnel that had collapsed, there was a fog of dust that had settled on the entire dimly-lit landscape of the rock-strewn side tunnel.

As they picked their way down into the recently collapsed tunnel, many of the timbers had fallen and partially obstructed their progress.

One of the timbers had pinned a prisoner to the floor of the tunnel, he was covered with coal dust and barely conscious.

As Jenz lifted the heavy beam, Ezekiel pulled the prisoner free.

At that moment the dust-covered prisoner came back to life and shouted, **"Get off me you Russian pig!"**

"Greta!" Zeke proclaimed.

"How would you know my name, you disgusting pig!"

Jenz threw the heavy beam aside and gently pulled Greta to her feet.

"Greta, are you hurt, can you walk?"

The dust-covered woman seemed confused in the dimly-lighted tunnel.

"Why do you care? Who are you?"

"Greta, it's your father and Ezekiel!"

"What! It is not possible. How could you be down in this terrible place?" She was sobbing as she spoke in German then in English. **"Am I dead or dreaming!"**

"We followed you. We would never give up until we found you. It is now time for us to follow the other prison mine-workers and get the hell out of here and get you to safety.

"Can you walk?"

"I'm not sure," whimpered Greta. She was crying.

"Oh, Dad! You should have let me die in the tunnel. I have been raped by a monster.

Jenz wiped her tears and gently picked her up. "You are alive. That is all that's important for me."

Jenz carefully carried Greta as Zeke led the way out of the collapsed tunnel and up through the main tunnel. They by-passed the shaky elevator and slowly climbed out of the main tunnel entrance.

Fresh air and bright sunlight acted like a tonic to Greta. Jenz set her down and she blinked rapidly, "I think I can walk. How did you both find me in this god-forsaken place?"

"Persistence." Zeke smiled as he quietly announced. As he observed her tear-steaked face, "Greta, your tears might have smeared your make-up!

"Oh, Ezekiel, thank you so much! I never thought I could smile again." She was still crying softly.

It was then that Jenz mentioned, "We aren't in Sudbury yet. Let's get into the warming-shed near the elevator and get you a little cleaned up and changed."

"Changed?" Sobbed Greta. "I have nothing to change into. They took all my outer clothing, even my undergarments in the Stasi prison in East Berlin. All I have are these rags."

Chapter 38

Finding Greta's Attacker

As they were shaking the dust out of their mining garments and coughing up coal dust, Jenz suggested, "Let's keep these mining clothes on and see if Greta could point out her attacker."

Greta chimed in. "Dad, wouldn't that be too risky? I just need to get as far away from this godforsaken dungeon as soon as possible."

Ezekiel had an even better idea. "Jenz, if Greta could quietly point the monster out among the guards and trustees that have congregated in the mine area, perhaps we could 'question' him here in the shed. Who knows, he may be apologetic and contrite." He finished his thought with a questioning smile.

"No matter the outcome," Zeke continued, "It might be beneficial for Greta's long term overall health. She has been through a very traumatic experience. This encounter she has lived through with this brutish guard has been even more atrocious and dreadful than her near rape from the Gestapo goons at her father's home in Nordhausen, Germany. I applaud her for being able to stay sane throughout this experience."

"Greta, Zeke is probably right. See if you can mingle with the crowd of prisoners out there and just point out the guard that attacked you. Don't try to lure him in here. Zeke and I can do that. Just point or nod to him to let us know which guard attacked you."

"Dad. I…don't know if I can do it. I… don't ever want to be within sight of that horrid man." She was trembling as she talked.

Jenz and Zeke tried to calm her down. "Don't worry, Greta. Your dad and I will be carefully watching. If that guard tries anything, he will have to deal with us."

After some hesitation, Greta walked out to the milling crowd on shaky legs. Her experience of being raped that morning, and then being pinned beneath a large timber deep in the mine, sent shivers down her spine. The bruise on her leg was going to be gigantic. Her body ached all over.

It was cool, but not quite cold. Even though it was early May, and the sun never set this time of year, the breeze intensified the chill that ran down her shoulders and back.

She was looking everywhere for the brutish guard who had attacked her earlier that morning. She remembered he was a large man with an ugly scar across his cheek which made a frightful countenance truly grotesque – almost beastly.

She wanted to stay in sight of the shed so Ezekiel and her dad could keep an eye on her and watch who she acknowledged as her attacker.

As she got closer to the crowd of prison miners, swarms of mosquitos and small gnats plagued her vision. The little critters swarmed around everyone's face. The bugs were getting in her ears, nose, and eyes, even under her clothing. She kept drifting deeper into the crowd and further from the shed and the safety of her dad and Ezekiel.

As Greta was thinking about retreating to the safety of the shed, someone put a vise-like grip of a fist on her arm above her elbow. The burly and powerful grip encircled her upper arm.

"There you are, my pretty prison-wife!"

Greta almost wretched at the sound of the brutish guard's mixed gutter-Russian voice. His giant hand had an unyielding grip on her arm. He spun her around and disoriented her so she could no longer see the warming-shed and safety.

The guard then ordered in a harsh and direct voice. **"Come, pretty one. We need to finish what we started this morning."**

"Leave me alone, or you will be sorry!" Shouted Greta in the smattering of Russian she could understand.

Smack! The guard hit the lithe Sudbury High School third-year student with an open fist across her face. He knocked her to the ground and broke and bloodied her nose.

The guard roughly picked her up and started to carry her off. Greta was stunned by the blow and found it impossible to resist being snatched up by the ugly beast.

In the meantime, Jenz and Ezekiel had lost sight of Greta and kept scanning the crowd, waiting for her to point out that morning's attacker.

Both men were about to exit the shed and look for Greta in the boisterous crowd of prisoners. Most of the minors were complaining about the swarms of mosquitos and wanted to get anywhere else for some midday rations.

"Wait!" Cried Zeke. "Someone is carrying what looks like Greta this way toward the shed. I think she is bleeding.

"This could be the guard who attacked her early this morning."

Jenz was boiling angry and enraged. Worse, yet, he hadn't had a decent meal since he left Berlin. He tried to calm himself and said to Zeke, "Let's conceal ourselves in the large lockers and see if this grisly guard is truly contrite."

While hiding in the locker, all Jenz could think about was how he was going to teach this brutish guard a lesson, and what he was going to have to eat when safely back to Sunday dinner with his all his family and Zeke's family at the Wayside Inn on the Post Road. Sudbury seemed like such a long way away at this point in his life. He blamed himself for the brutality that had come to Greta and his family.

This was an unfortunate set of circumstances for the guard who burst into the shed with the gruff cacophonous tone, **"Now my pretty prison-wife, we will finish our morning's fun!"**

Chapter 39

Confronting a Rapist

Ezekiel, as he was looking through a crack in the locker door, could see the brutish guard thrust Greta into the shed and onto the rough hard wooden floor. It looked to him that Greta's nose had been broken, there was blood all over her face. Although he was ready to jump out of the locker and get between the guard and Greta, he thought her father might like to make the first move.

The guard threw Greta onto the un-swept and filthy floor of the shed and proceeded to drop his pants. He climbed on top of Greta with a warning.

"It will do you no good to cry out. No one will hear you or pay attention to you. I am in charge here."

At that moment, Jenz quietly opened the cramped locker door and stood behind the guard. The brute was oblivious to the presence of anyone else in the room; he was too busy attempting to continue his morning rape of a defenseless high-school-aged woman. Meanwhile, Zeke had opened his locker and joined Jenz. Both men were incensed as they looked at each other and at the monster on top of Greta.

At that moment Greta glanced upward and noticed her father and Ezekiel moving to get behind her rapist. A smile spread over her face and all the pain seemed to melt away.

The guard noticed his victim's smile and grinned showing misaligned, yellowing, decayed, and missing teeth as he grunted, **"Ah, you are enjoying this, eh?"**

In one swift motion Jenz grabbed the guard by his hair and the back of his shirt. He gave a sudden yank upward and jerked the guard off Greta; Ezekiel covered her with a towel from the locker which had concealed him. Zeke noticed that Greta had already lost weight. She looked pale, bruised, and thin.

The guard was incensed, and cried out.

"What are you doing! This is my woman; I am in charge here!" He was a swinish degenerative-beast of a man.

"Sadly," Jenz related in a firm, but even tone. **"You are not in charge of anyone anymore!"**

Slap! Jenz issued a strong slap across the guard's face which sent the brute sprawling to the floor of the dilapidated warming-shed. The slap was so firm, it broke the monster's jaw.

It reminded Jenz of the blow he had delivered to the ant-Semantic bully in his grade-school years when the ruffian had disrespected and was beating up his childhood friend, Ezekiel.

Jenz immediately went over and roughly picked up the guard by an arm and hit him hard on the back of his neck right at the base of the skull with the side of his closed fist. **Snap!** Jenz could hear one or more vertebrae fracture under the blow.

Ever since his teenage years, Jenz had no idea how strong he really was, or how his strength could help him minimize the intimidation and cruelty of the Gestapo with his friends and family.

As the guard struggled to get to his feet, he found his legs wouldn't support him anymore. His arms couldn't even push his body off the filth-ridden floor. His broken neck must have damaged his spinal cord. Although fully conscious and breathing, the brute was reduced to a sniveling idiot. Even his speech was garbled, Jenz wasn't sure if it was the broken condylar head of his lower jaw, or his broken neck that wouldn't allow the guard to speak coherently any longer.

Ezekiel commented, "Jenz, you made short work of a rather large and imposing monster. What should we do with him?" I think the ground is still frozen from the winter, so it would be difficult to bury him."

"Greta," her dad asked. "Are you okay? What would **you** suggest we do to this very poor excuse for human refuse?"

The whimpering guard on the floor could only stare at the women he still wanted to possess. His pleading looks from his glazed eyes could not comprehend what was happening to his damaged body.

Greta replied, "I know you had dispatched some of the Gestapo creeps in the Rhine. But we are a long way from northern Germany.

"Also, one of the earlier criminals who came into our home in Sudbury, found himself locked in the trunk of his own automobile with the top part of his head missing."

Ezekiel spoke up. "I think our degenerate vegetable has had an accident and found himself in the coal mine at the bottom of the elevator shaft."

Jenz and Ezekiel were pretty sure the guard didn't understand their language, but he seemed to be able to sense his fate. There was a look of abject terror in his eyes. He kept repeating the phrase, *nyet, nyet zek; nyet, nyet zek* (no, no; not prisoner). His other mutterings were probably a curious mix of Russian swears.

Jenz and Ezekiel pulled up the lout's pants and started to walk him out of the shed while balancing him between them. Basically, they were carrying him because his arms hung loosely at his side and his legs would no longer work but could only drag limply along behind him on the dirt-encrusted floor.

"Greta," Jenz called out over his shoulder, "Zeke and I will be back shortly, sweetheart. Get dressed as best you can. We will find you a warm shower and some decent food soon."

"Hold up, please!" exclaimed Greta. "You aren't going anywhere without me. I am not, even for a minute, staying here where I might be found!"

"Okay, sweetheart. Wrap a towel around your head and keep this handkerchief over your nose, I'm afraid it might be broken," replied her father.

Jenz and Ezekiel perp-walked the guard over to the entrance of elevator shaft with Greta trailing a pace or two behind. There was a mix of fog and coal dust percolating out of the mine through the elevator shaft.

As they neared the opening, it was obvious the elevator itself was at the bottom of the mine.

The guard started moaning. *Nyet, nyet, nyet…* As they looked down the abyss, the guard tried to break away. By suddenly forcing his head forward he slipped out of their grasp and tumbled into the elevator shaft.

All they heard was a rumble-rumble and the brutes dying scream as he finally thumped to the bottom of the mine.

After disposing of the guard, Jenz and Ezekiel cleaned up as best they could in the crude warming-shed and got into their Russian officer uniforms. Jenz place the transfer papers for their prisoner to be transferred to the Moscow prison in his Russian Officer's tunic.

"Greta, how is your face feeling?" Zeke asked.

"It's pretty sore, I might have a couple of chipped teeth."

"Your bleeding seems to have stopped, but it may take a while for your swelling and bruising to subside. It will probably get worse, before it starts to heal."

Jenz then added, "Greta, I have to tie your hands together. We are going directly to your hut and then to the front entrance of this chamber of torture they call a prison and submit our transfer papers to the warden. I need his signature for your release to the prison in Moscow."

Jenz and Ezekiel had to support and almost carry Greta as they slowly walked toward her hut. Most of the guards and prisoners were on their way to the noon meal, but few of the men would even dare to look at the two Russian officers dragging a woman prisoner with her arms tied together.

"Dad, I have to ask you a question."

"What is it, Greta?"

"How do you propose to get us out of this very remote prison and back to civilization?"

"Ezekiel and I are two Russian Senior Officers tasked with our orders to bring a prisoner back to Butyrka prison in Moscow for intense interrogation."

Greta then asked with some trepidation, "Could you take back two prisoners?"

"What!" Exclaimed Zeke.

"Why two?" Jenz asked. "Our orders specifically mention only one prisoner."

Chapter 40

The Sasha Problem

As Jenz and Ezekiel each had hold of one of Greta's arms, they helped carry and support her legs as they transported her back to her hut.

Ezekiel asked, "Greta, what are you talking about?"

Jenz added, "Have you any idea of the difficulties we may have to face just to get out of this godforsaken, desolate country?"

Greta asked in a clear and precise voice. "Would it be any more difficult than getting me out of Nazi Germany as your aide?"

Jenz and Zeke just looked at each other. Jenz did a bit of an eye-roll.

"Just who is this other prisoner?" Zeke questioned.

"She was a student at the university in Leningrad when she was arrested with a group of other students for protesting the university's food policy.

"Her name is Sasha, and she is the only person here who has been helpful in getting me through the brutal rapes that are perpetrated on almost all the female prisoners. She works in the prison kitchen; she has been more than kind to me.

"Her boyfriend was shot in the head for telling the secret police that arresting Sasha on such flimsy charges was ridiculous. He was shot in the head right in front of Sasha and many other witnesses from her university. His blood splashed all over Sasha.

"Her parents live in Berlin, near the Tiergarten Park. She has been in this god-forgotten gulag for over a year and because she is young, she is continually raped by some of the most brutal guards in this prison of horrors."

"Can you trust this Sasha person completely?" Jenz asked.

"Dad." Greta continued. "She has told me she has never heard from her parents and they probably have no idea what has happened to her. If we could get her back to her loved ones in Berlin, it would completely redirect her life. She would like to enter politics and be a voice for changing the circumstances of women everywhere, including the slave-labor prisoners in the Russian Gulags."

"What do you think, Zeke?"

"Well," Zeke suggested. "I think we are up against two bright and very determined women. To be truthful, I never thought Greta could pull off her 'aide' impersonation and safely get us out of the Reich during the last gasps of the war.

"If Sasha could act as if she didn't want to leave the security of prison life here to be taken by two Russian Officers to be thoroughly interrogated in another very secure prison in Moscow, we may, possibly, be successful in getting them both out of this gulag here in Vorkuta.

"It is a risk all four of us would have to undertake. In addition, we would have to change the perception of the warden here to convince him we have discovered additional evidence implicating this other prisoner in Greta's crimes.

"We would have to lead them both out of here in shackles and they would both have to act convincingly that they were not happy about being dragged to another prison in Moscow for intense interrogation."

Chapter 41

Difficulty Exiting Vorkuta Gulag

Jenz and Ezekiel first dragged Greta directly over to her hut and talked with the *starosta*. * Both men wanted to be sure this woman knew exactly what was going on with one of her prison underlings.

By informing the *starosta* of the change in circumstances for the prisoner, it showed her a degree of respect for what both officers hoped was cooperation.

Ezekiel tried to explain to the *starosta* that he and the Colonel were taking the prisoner back to the Moscow for "proper interrogation." Although the *starosta* avoided any but cursory eye contact, she did seem to be cooperative.

Zeke asked in his broken Russian, "*Starosta,* can the prisoner get cleaned up? She must retain her wrist restraints because she has been known to be dangerous."

The *starosta* complied by handing Greta a clean towel and a fresh prison uniform. In return, Jenz showed her the transfer papers, knowing she probably couldn't read or understand them. However, the woman kept running her fingers over the embossed NKVD seal. She certainly under stood that particular mark of fear and intimidation.

Jenz then asked a more personal question in a calm and direct voice. "*Starosta,* could you please tell me your name?"

---

*A *starosta* was in charge of each barrack. Their main task was to resolve fights, ensure peace and tranquility in the hut, to greet new prisoners, and ensure everyone had a place to sleep. They would also inform the guards if there was any possible prisoner uprisings, chicanery, or other difficulty with the orderly running of the prison barracks.

For a senior Red Army officer to ask a prisoner his or her name could mean only one thing. Trouble for the prisoner; so Jenz added, "I would like to inform the Warden of your cooperation."

"Thank you. My name is Evana," replied the woman.

Then Ezekiel confronted the *starosta* directly. "Miss Evana, our investigation has uncovered the name of another prisoner who may be connected to the crime we are investigating.

"Is that prisoner a resident in this barrack?" Evana asked quickly.

"We are not sure," Jenz answered truthfully. "We think she may work in the kitchen clean-up area. She goes by the name Sasha. We need to interrogate her immediately."

"I will go there directly and if I can locate her, I will bring her here." Evana spoke in broken Russian.

"Please do not tell her that we are here to arrest her, Evana. She may get resistive and try to flee from the area." Jenz smiled and clapped the *starosta* on the back.

After the *starosta* had left the hut, Jenz and Ezekiel counseled Greta on how both women should react when under 'arrest' while trying to exit the slave-labor gulag.

Both Jenz and Ezekiel wanted to make sure both women knew that they might be slapped around a bit or spoken to harshly in order to let the warden and guards know they were under arrest and facing severe consequences.

After about a forty-minute wait, Evana and the "suspect" Sasha entered Greta's barrack.

Sasha was clearly shocked at seeing the two Red Army Officers and Greta in shackles waiting by the stove at the end of the hut.

Hopefully, her facial expression and obvious shock registered with the *starosta* as surprise of not knowing what was in store for her.

Greta called out to her. "Sasha, say nothing to anyone, or it might go badly for both of us!"

Ezekiel spoke to her in harsh terms in German so the starosta would not understand. **"Zet Sasha. You are under arrest by the East German Government. We need to place you in shackles in order to transport you out of this prison to a secure prison in Moscow."**

As Zeke approached Sasha with the shackles, he almost whispered in German so no one else could hear. "Don't be alarmed Fräulein, we are trying to get you home to your family."

As they departed for the main gate, Jenz said good-bye to the *starosta* by a compliment. "Thank you for your assistance, *Starosta* Evana. I will see that the warden knows of your service and cooperation."

It was getting late in the afternoon but the sun was still high from the horizon. They had to walk almost a mile back to the warden's office near the main entrance of the prison.

Much of the way both men almost had to carry Greta by bracing each of her arms because of her shacky legs and slow gait. They had to walk around several spongy-wet areas and small puddles that were forming as the surface permafrost had begun to melt in the continuous sunshine.

During the walk, Jenz explained to Greta and Sasha, "Please ladies, do not say anything in the warden's presence or to the guards at the front gate. We will let Zeke muddle through with his broken Russian with his German accent.

"Please forgive Zeke and me if we appear strident or impolite. We might have to slap you around a bit, but we will not connect with your face. Remember, you are dangerous prisoners we are taking for special interrogation!"

Once in the warden's office, Zeke expressed his thanks for the warden's hospitality and kindness in directing them to the hotel. He again displayed the official papers they were carrying for the prison transfer and asked the warden to sign and stamp the bottom of the document while talking in his broken Russian.

During the signing process, Ezekiel explained to the warden his appreciation for the *starosta* in the prisoner's barracks for ferreting out another prisoner who was also tainted and wanted by the **NKVD** for similar crimes as the original prisoner.

When Greta started to complain in German for the tightness of her restraints and holding up her arms, Jenz took a mighty swing at her and connected with the back of her shirt off her shoulder. Greta flung herself to the floor amid a torrent of German and Russian curses and the cruelty of the Russian prison system.

Sasha immediately went over to help her up and comfort her.

"Warden, I will be sure to mention your cooperation in this prisoner transfer to the prison authorities in Moscow. My colleagues at the **NKVD** will hear of your advice and cooperation. Your service to our Motherland is exemplary and they will know of it."

Jenz seemed to understand and did a bit of an eye-roll.

The warden expressed his thanks and in halting Russian offered to escort them to the *vakta* (guardhouse).

At the guardhouse, the warden raised his hand with four fingers extended and a horse-drawn wagon materialized to take them back to the Hotel Tsentralnaya.

Chapter 42

The Challenging Journey Home

The evening after their release, Greta had a chance to get into a warm shower to rid most of the grime and coal dust from her body and some dust out of her lungs. Sasha was able to get some of the prison smell off her body.

Once they were in the hotel room, Sasha started to thank Jenz and Ezekiel for getting her released but Zeke immediately held up his hand and pointed to the ceiling. **"You both are under the detention of the Red Army. Do not try anything that would cause us to have to harm you on the way to your prison in Moscow!"**

Jenz didn't want to get them any clothes other than some undergarments. They wanted everyone to understand they were transporting two prisoners to the Butyrka Prison in the Central District in Moscow.

Dinner was a quiet celebration in their hotel room. When the food was delivered to their room, Greta and Sasha were trussed up like Christmas Turkeys and tied to chairs for the food delivery person to observe.

The train left the next morning for the three-day journey to Moscow. Jenz and Zeke couldn't chance sending a message home to Ilse or Adiya until they returned to West Berlin. No one knew who might be listening or reading their message.

There were very few passengers on the train back to Moscow, but the rouse of the officers transporting two prisoners had to be maintained. Greta, however, slept fitfully with almost continuous nightmares.

One day out of Moscow one of the train officers started to show an overt interest in our "prisoners." It was pretty evident he was an **NKVD** officer. He spoke in Russian, but Zeke could understand most of what he had to say. This "secret police" officer was tall, at least six feet, with a fair degree of muscle mass. I certainly didn't want to take him on.

"Gentlemen. I see you are transporting two felons. Are they dangerous?"

Ezekiel answered in German-accented broken Russian and explained that we were both officers from East Germany stationed in Berlin. "Our prisoners are not dangerous, as long as they are restrained."

"Could I trouble you for her papers?" The overly polite NKVD officer seemed a little too interested in a routine prison transfer. He kept looking at our uniforms and scratching his head.

My immediate thought was that he found something confusing about our uniforms or ribbons. The ribbons showed that we had been involved in the great Russian Red Army advancement to the Vistula and on to Berlin in 1945.

The first sign of trouble with this officer began slowly. "May I see your prisoner's papers?" This NKVD officer was subtle and polite, but more than a little persistent.

I could sense Ezekiel's nervous concern, so I stood and produced a portfolio from underneath my tunic.

As I produced the papers, I suggested, "Sir, since there are other passengers in this train carriage, could we go somewhere where I could spread the papers out for proper examination?"

I motioned to the rear of the next carriage and suggested that the officer follow me. I held up one finger for Zeke as a wait signal. I mentioned to Ezekiel, "Keep a watchful eye on our prisoners. Do not let them free of their shackles, even if they need to eat or use the bathroom."

The NKVD officer followed me to the next train carriage. Since there were still a few passengers in that car, I kept walking to the carriage that contained only a couple of prisoners and one guard. The prisoners were all shackled to their seats. The one guard was at the rear of the car, but there was a table in the first row away from the shackled detainees.

I sat at the table and proceeded to spread out the prison transfer papers. The officer sat beside me and started to examine the paperwork. He continuously ran his fingers over the raised NKVD seal.

In an instant it became clear to me that this police officer was going to be trouble.

His first words in heavily accented German confirmed our difficulties. **"These papers are bogus. Counterfeit. They are signed by our department head who died two years ago!"**

"My good man," I replied in a Russian-German kind voice, "I am sure you are mistaken. We received these orders from Colonel Paplovich from the East German Consulate just last week."

"Impossible!" Bellowed the unsuspecting and hapless officer.

At that point in our conversation, I asked the gentleman to "Please look closer. I pointed with the finger of my left hand to the seal on the bottom of the paperwork.

As the officer was sitting down and squinting at the seal, I immediately stood up an brought my full weight behind the side of my closed fist to a blow to the back of the officer's skull.

Crack!

The blow stunned the NKVD officer. His forehead hit the hard wooden table and splashed blood all over the paperwork.

I carefully sat down and placed my forearm around the unfortunate officer's neck. We were shielded from the other prisoners and guard by the backs of the wooden seats.

I gave the officer a quick and hard squeeze on his neck. I could hear his hyoid bone and mandible crack under the pressure. I then applied continuous firm pressure to the officer's throat and neck.

He cried out once, but any sound was camouflaged by the noisy train as it moved down the tracks toward Moscow.

I left the NKVD officer curled up on the seat and went to the back of the train to talk with the guard. I knew almost all the citizens of the Soviet Union had a special hatred of these "secret police" officers. These officers instilled an almost constant fear and trepidation to all citizens in Russia.

"Sir." I began. "Could you help me with an NKVD officer who has had an unfortunate accident?"

My East German accent was a little rusty and my Russian was worse. When I pulled out a shiny U.S. silver dollar, however, he seemed to immediately understand.

I motioned for him to follow me with a wave of a finger. The table was a bit of a mess. It was covered with vomit and blood.

I eased the NKVD officer out of the seat and the guard grabbed the other arm. We brought him to the space between the railroad carriages.

I removed the man's wallet and offered the Rubles to the guard, who didn't refuse the generous offer. As I watched the desolate landscape slide by, I gently eased the dead officer onto the tracks between the speeding cars.

I thanked the guard for his help. When we returned to the carriage and approached the blood-spattered table, I motioned for the guard to clean up the mess with a towel. I waved my hand across the air above the table. Although at first, he didn't seem to understand; he immediately grasped the situation when I placed another silver dollar on the table.

We received a lot of severe glances, dirty looks, and moments of incredulity as we transitioned from the train to the large Sheremetyevo

Airdrome just about twenty kilometers north-west of the center of Moscow.

The sideward glances were perhaps because of our Russian Uniforms. We had purchased large sunglasses, hats, and comfortable clothing for Greta and Sasha. We no longer pretended she was a prisoner, and unshackled their wrists.

At the Airdrome we purchased four round-trip tickets to Krakow's Balice Airport, just outside of Krakow, Poland. This airport was then run by the Polish Military. One-way tickets would have immediately raised questions we didn't have time to answer.

While at the airport in Krakow, we purchased four round-trip tickets to Schönefeld Airport outside of East Berlin. We were all dog-tired from the stress of looking over our shoulder during the entire egress from the Gulag at Vorkuta. Perhaps we let our guard slip a little too early.

Chapter 43

Relaxing a Little Too Soon

Nothing too surprising happened on our journey from Moscow to the airport in Poland. We had to keep up the guise of transporting prisoners to East Berlin. Both women were still in shackles and looked pretty tired and beat.

Greta looked miserable, even though she was almost free. Her nose bled periodically and it looked like every inch of her body was bruised. Both women looked so tired they could hardly stand.

As we were going through customs, one of the officials asked to see our tickets and papers. The custom officer looked like a mild-mannered functionary until he opened his mouth.

The official asked in firmly Russian-accented German, **"Gentlemen I need to examine your papers for the prisoners."**

Ezekial asked if were customary to question senior Russian Officers and heroes of the war.

"Sir!" The official-looking functionary retorted. "We have had a message from the NKVD to be on the lookout for two female prisoners who had not shown up at the Butyrka Prison in Moscow.

"Now I find two female persons in shackles who have come to our city and have tickets, round-trip tickets no less, to the Airdrome in East Berlin. Something doesn't smell right to me!"

Jenz spoke up with an appropriate Russian-accented German, "Sir, please let me explain to you and show you our complete paperwork. Is there a place where we can talk without interference from the curious public? I am sure these orders will clarify everything for you."

"All of you, come with me!" Commanded the customs agent.

The agent led us through the customs check area to a small room off to the side of the passageway to the aircraft. Many passengers were getting ready to board the aircraft. Some were walking out of the double doors out to the waiting planes.

The room was really too small for everyone so Ezekiel asked if should wait outside with the prisoners. Jenz went in with the customs agent and spread out his paperwork on the small desk. The agent locked the door from the inside with a key.

"As you can see from our orders, Sir," Jenz began in a very polite and smooth tone that was almost condescending.

"We have orders to transport two criminals from the corrective labor camp at Vorkuta to our offices in East Berlin. You can see from the embossed seal of the NKVD that our orders are accurate and compelling."

The custom agent functionary sat down and pulled out a large magnifying glass from the middle drawer of the desk and examined our orders

After a few minutes, the agent said "Ah huh! These orders are not accurate. They are fake. Look at these ink-bleeds! I am calling security."

As the agent reached over the desk to push an alarm button Jenz grabbed his arm and suggested, "Please, agent, I don't recommend you do that!"

"Why not!" The agent shot back as he reached with his other hand to push the alarm button.

Since the agent was getting agitated and quite loud, Jenz thought it best to quiet the meddlesome functionary as quickly as possible.

As the agent was reaching with his other hand for the alarm button, Jenz rendered a quick blow to the unsuspecting agents throat crushing his larynx. That seemed to quiet him down. As Jenz placed him in a choke-hold and gradually squeezed the life out of him Jenz thought he should at least explain his quixotic actions.

"Sir," he started. "I have just rescued my daughter and her friend from a slave-labor camp in Siberia. My friend Ezekiel and I are going to make sure they arrive safely at their respective homes. It is important that they get to see their friends and loved ones again. Unfortunately, because of your foolishness here today, I cannot say the same for you."

Jens then took the key from the deceased agent's pocket, propped him the chair, unlocked the door from the inside, and locked it from the outside.

After locking the door from the outside, he worked the key back and forth until it snapped in the lock ensuring it would be a while before anyone could discover the missing customs agent.

Immediately after landing in East Berlin and clearing customs, Ezekiel told the women to go into the Ladies room and remove their shackles. "Please leave any shackles in the trash."

Both officers removed their officer jackets and immediately placed them on the women as they exited the bathroom.

We then went to the closest kiosk and purchased hats, scarfs, and sunglasses for the newly arrived and free women.

Ezekiel asked the cab driver waiting at the curb, "Please take us to the nicest and closest hotel in the western part of the city."

The driver took us to a quiet West Berlin hotel. the Hotel Berlin was not too far from the Tiergarten. We chose a two-room suite so Greta and Sasha could have their own room.

After we closed the hotel room door, Sasha broke down into tears. She and Greta were tearfully hugging and thanking Ezekiel and me when I suggested Sasha might want to call her parents.

"Oh, thank you, Jenz and Ezekiel. They do not live too far from here."

Sasha's parents were heartbroken when they heard about her captivity in Siberia and her boyfriend's sudden murder. They had been trying to get information from the Soviet Embassy in Berlin for over a year with no success.

They were sickened when they saw Greta and heard her story. They had no idea that the Soviet Union even had anything like the slave-labor-work camps. Greta's bruised and battered face, broken nose, and shaved head gave them some idea of what their daughter, Sasha, had experienced.

Chapter 44

⊸•◦∽◦•⊶

A Surprise Visit from Captain Seth Dobrinsky

The next morning, we had a surprise visit from Dr. Dobrinsky from the Raytheon Board of Directors. He was currently stationed at the Naval War College in Newport, Rode Island, and worked closely with the FBI and Office of Naval Intelligence.

Captain Dobrinsky evidently had been trying to get information about the abduction and kidnapping of my daughter, Greta, and had followed us until we disappeared into the Soviet Union. He had lots of questions and wanted answers.

He mentioned that the FBI had been working to protect the Sidewinder missile case and had issued arrest warrants for Gerold Semanski of Harris Street in Revere, and several of the Russian thugs that had been associated with the address on John Street in Jamaica Plain. Since the home at 2031 John Street, Jamacia Plain was no longer there, they were having trouble finding the Russians that had initially held Greta.

"My apology, Captain. I'm afraid my daughter was responsible for the little mishap that leveled and burned that property to the ground."

"By golly, Ramsgrund. Did Greta know how dangerous those men were to her safety?"

Zeke spoke up. "I think she had a pretty good idea, Captain. She was a little steamed after being kidnapped directly from her Sudbury High School and locked in the trunk of their car for a few hours."

"But Gentlemen." Continued Captain Dobrinsky. "Did your daughter have any munitions training?"

"Just from my stories of my difficulties in Hamburg during the war," Jenz interjected.

"It is remarkable that she wasn't killed in the explosion and the ensuing firestorm that reduced the structure to ashes."

The captain then looked around the hotel room and remarked, "By the way, where is Greta now?"

"This is a two-room suite, captain. She is in her room. I would be happy to get her, but you must understand she has been through quite a perilous experience. Please do not look alarmed by her condition," admonished Jenz.

"Of course not, Mr. Ramsgrund. She was only gone less than two weeks; her plight cannot be too awful. "Besides," continued the captain, "I have seen a lot of traumas in my career with the naval intelligence department."

"I will bring her out for you to question," Jenz added. "Please do not say anything about her appearance."

After a few minutes, Greta came limping out hanging on to her father. She was completely bald. Her bloodshot eyes were in black sockets set deep on a badly bruised and swollen face. Her nose was crushed to one side of her face. Her lower jaw looked misaligned. She was bent over and in obvious pain and bleeding from her mouth.

"Oh, my dear heavens!" Captain Dobrinsky exclaimed. **"What did they do to you?"** He felt lightheaded and stumbled backward into a chair, then he immediately vomited onto the floor.

Greta pointed to her father and opened and closed her hand.

Jenz explained to the captain. "Greta would be happy to tell you when she can talk better. She would like me to outline what happened to her. Sweetheart, let me take you back to your room so you can rest."

When Jenz came out of Greta's bedroom, Captain Dobrinsky couldn't be apologetic enough.

"I am so sorry, Ramsgrund. I know the FBI will want facial photographs for their file. I will call for a photographer and have this documented fully. With your permission, of course.

"Did the beating she suffered break or damage her leg?"

"No." Offered Zeke. "Her leg was damaged with the collapse of a tunnel deep underground in a coal mine."

"Oh, dear God," stammered Captain Dobrinsky. "This just keeps getting worse!

"The state department will want to know about this. I am sure our representative to Russia would be very concerned that this cowardly and brutal beating, suffered by your beautiful daughter, could lead to even further difficulties between our countries and possibly cause an international incident."

Ezekiel responded. "Unfortunately, it does get much worse, captain."

"How could it get worse, gentlemen, unless she was killed?"

Jenz pointed at Zeke and nodded.

In a subdued voice Ezekiel explained.

"She was repeatedly raped by the guards at the Vorkuta Gulag, captain."

I thought the good captain was going to vomit again, but he ran into the bathroom and slammed the door. We could hear him wretch and loose the rest of whatever had been in his stomach.

Chapter 45

A Subdued Homecoming

We tried to get Greta's broken teeth restored in West Berlin, but she couldn't open her mouth wide enough for the dentist to accomplish much treatment. The doctor was able to polish off some of the sharp angles of the jagged teeth that were causing the bleeding on her tongue; he felt so concerned about Greta's overall condition, that he didn't charge for the emergency visit.

We were met on the aircraft, shortly after it landed in Boston by a representative from the state department and two naval petty officers in uniform. The navel insignias indicated they were members of the shore patrol. They came directly on to the plane from a state department vehicle that arrived at the plane the minute the stairway was brought to the aircraft.

Greta had, thankfully, slept most of the flight. She didn't even awaken during our refueling stop in Greenland.

We were all surprised when the well-over six-foot representative from the state department ducked into the plane and addressed us in our first-class cabin seats.

"Misters Ramsgrund and Leven, I am agent Vishinski from the department of state for Soviet affairs, please come with us. We have a dedicated room in the airport for you to meet your families." Then he paused. "By the way, where is your daughter?"

"She is asleep under the blanket," Jenz replied. "I will wake her and help her off the plane."

Mr. Vishinski had a color photograph of Greta from her high-school yearbook. He showed it to the two petty officers so they could verify the girl they were there to protect and transfer safely to her home in Sudbury.

Jenz uncovered his daughter and gently pushed her shoulder in order to waken her. As her dad was helping her out of the seat, Mr. Vishinski and the two petty officers got a good look at Greta.

Mr. Vishinski's rather impolitic comment was blurted out. **"What the hell happened to your daughter!"**

Both petty officers started weeping. **"Oh my God!"** Exclaimed Benson, the senior chief petty officer. "Who could do such a thing?"

"Gentlemen." Ezekiel began, "Greta is one of the lucky ones to escape from the Vorkuta Gulag. Most of the other thousands of slave-prisoners in that Siberian prison are probably stuck there for the rest of their lives.

"Even though Greta was only in Vorkuta for a short period of time, what you see on the outside of her body is only the tip of the iceberg of what happened to this innocent girl."

The rest of the homecoming seemed to go relatively smoothly. Even though most of her family held back their tears, it was obvious that seeing Greta's physical condition was heart-rendering for everyone.

When Ezekiel's daughter, and Greta's best friend, Chasha, went to hug Greta, both women burst into tears.

Greta whimpered and tried to speak through her tears. "Oh, Chasha, in addition to hurting all over, you shouldn't hug me. I feel like so much damaged goods!"

"What are you talking about, dear Greta?"

"I don't think I will ever recover from being brutally raped by a monstrous Russian guard at the Vorkuta Gulag." She moaned. "My dad should have left me to die in the bottom of the prison coal mine."

"Oh Greta," cried Chasha. You are home now with family. You are safe now."

"Chasha, I will never feel safe again!

Chapter 46

❧❦❧

Back to Classes

The day after Greta, Zeke, and I returned home my wife, Ilsa, thought we should let Greta sleep late. She was in no condition to go right back to school. However, she came downstairs into our kitchen just after eight O'clock and had breakfast with us.

"Greta, I am surprised to see you up this early, I thought you would like to take a few days off in order to heal a bit before you resumed your studies at the high school."

"Thanks, Dad, but I don't want to miss any more school."

Ilse then asked a delicate question. "Are you sure you feel up to it, dear? Are you okay on the stairs?"

"I think so. As long as the stairs have a hand-rail to grasp. I might bring the cane I found in the cellar for stability.

"I have to be in school; I don't want to get too far behind in my classes, and I have to catch up on plenty of assignments. But it would be helpful if I could find a crutch, a hat or wig, sunglasses and plenty of your make-up, Mom. I don't want to scare the kids or my teachers."

I then had to ask. "Greta, would it be okay if I talked with your principal, Mister Jacobson? I would like to fill him in on what you have experienced in East Berlin and in the Vorkuta Gulag, before you show up at the school."

"Please don't call him, Dad. I want to explain to the principal, my teachers, and my classmates exactly what I went through at the hands of some criminal Americans and the brutal situation at Vorkuta.

"I was thinking when I awoke early this morning, that it might be important, perhaps for my own mental health, that I ask the principal if we could have an assembly after lunch tomorrow.

"It is important I get through this very demeaning and terrifying time in my life on my own. Except..."

"Except what?" Ilsa immediately questioned in a caring and loving tone.

"Except, I know I won't be alone.

"Chasha said she would be with me and tell our class-mates some of the gruesome experiences she went through at Treblinka during the Nazi occupation of our homeland."

"Would she agree to do something like that?" Jenz queried. "Talking about her time in Warsaw and at Treblinka might bring back some terrible nightmares."

"She has already agreed to join me. It would be important that you and her parents, and as many other parents who wanted to listen to our story, come and join us.

"Also, because your company was such a help for us financially and giving you paid time from work, anyone at Raytheon would also be invited and welcome to join us at the school assembly.

"After all, dad, you and mom and Adiya and Ezekiel have been our inspiration. Chasha and I know we owe our lives to you and Ezekiel. Chasha and I also know what you and Ezekiel did for all of us in Germany who weren't Nazis during the war."

This was the first time I had heard Greta use the first names of my close friends Zeke and Adiya. I thought to myself, good Lord, my daughter has become an adult. She was only away from her school for two weeks!

The petite little waif Zeke and I first met in a restaurant in Nordhausen three short years ago has been transformed before my eyes into a very strong woman.

"Greta." I asked. "Are you sure you both feel strong enough to stand in front of your classmates and teachers and bare some quite personal secrets from your past, our past?"

"I may have to sit before my classmates, teachers and parents, but I know the man upstairs will look after us."

Chapter 47

A Memorable High School Assembly

Icalled Ezekiel from the office the next day so I could clue him in on what our daughters had planned. He had heard all about it and told me the principal had agreed to hold the assembly, but it would have to wait an extra day until Friday at 1 pm.

I was treated a bit like a hero by my boss, Jerry Lobell, and Doctor Clemson, our head of the Avionics Department. The head of security, Mr. Hammond even came by my desk to ask how Greta was getting along. I invited them all to the assembly that was going to be held the next afternoon. They had all heard about and indicated they were coming.

I wasn't sure how many parents or folks from Raytheon would show up, but the parking lot was overflowing when we arrived at the school Friday afternoon. People were parked all over Sudbury Center and even in the surrounding churches and into the town cemetery.

Ilse and I found Zeke as we walked into the school. Adiya was already in the school auditorium saving our seats in the third row.

After we took our seats, I asked Adyia and Zeke, "When did our daughters become adults and such strong women?"

"It happened so fast, we almost missed it, Jenz. I am astonished they are strong enough women to pull this off!"

"I think they might have been trying to protect their mental health. It means a lot that they would plan and attempt this almost confession of their past. I don't think anyone at the school knows their history – except that they are post-war refugees from Europe."

The lights dimmed and two women walked, one limped, out to a set of chairs in the center of the stage.

Chasha began and did much of the talking. Greta had long pants, a hat, and a cotton scarf on a warm Friday afternoon in May.

"Good afternoon, friends and families. This is the second year my friend Greta and I have attended Sudbury High School. None of you have any idea how grateful we are to be here.

"Many of you know my mother, Adiya. What you may not know is that she is really my older sister. Both of our parents were killed by the Nazis two months after they attacked Poland on the 1st of September 1939. My older sister, Adiya took care of me when our parents were shot in our home in Warsaw and we were forced to move into the Jewish Ghetto, a walled-off section of the capital city.

"The Nazi troops from the Wehrmacht severely limited the amount of food allowed into the Getto for several months. This was an effort to starve the inhabitants into submission.

"This starvation tactic was taking too long for Hitler and his henchmen, the SS, so on the 15 of April the army broke down the ghetto walls and forced the polish citizens to the center of the city where the railroad station was located. Anyone too old or two young to move to the rail station was shot or killed immediately.

"Those of us that were lucky enough to get to the rail station were forced into rail-cars used to transport cattle. The Nazis packed one to two hundred people in each cattle car with no food or water, or toilet facilities for the sixty-five-kilometer trip to Treblinka.

"Of course, no one had any idea what Treblinka was all about. We were told we were being transported to the conquered territories in the east to do farm work.

"Once we arrived at Treblinka, the Nazis made us wait in the hot unventilated train cars for the rest of the day without food or water.

"After they unloaded the cattle cars, several of my friends and neighbors, especially the elderly, were deceased from dehydration.

"I'm telling you all this, because this is how I first met my step-dad, Ezekiel.

"Greta's dad and Ezekiel were both Jews impersonating German officers. Greta's father was dressed in an SS uniform, Ezekiel was dressed as a Wehrmacht sergeant. They were at the Treblinka camp to procure workers for their secret rocket camp in northern Germany.

"Immediately after unloading the cattle cars all of us were herded into a separation area. The women and children went to the left and all the men went to the right. All of us were told to completely disrobe in order to get into the showers. We were told we needed to shower and get deloused before being transferred to farmland in the Eastern Territories.

"Greta's dad, Jenz Ramsgrund and my dad came into the women's undressing area when we were all completely naked and told the Nazi officer that their secret weapons plant in the north of Germany needed women for weapon assembly.

"When my big sister, now my mom, Adiya asked my dad, masquerading as a Wehrmacht sergeant, what was happening to them, she was brutally whipped by one of the Ukrainian guards. She still has a florid red scar on her back that has not ever completely healed.

"I see my mom in the third row. Mom, would you mind coming up here for a moment and showing my friends and classmates your back?"

As Adiya came onto the stage, she remarked, "Of course not, dear sister.

Adiya t hen dropped her shirt down enough to show an ugly red welt of a scar from her neck to almost her waist. The scar was purply red and angry looking.

Thank you, dear sister.

"My future dad...

"My future dad grabbed the whip out of the guard's hand and firmly told the guard that he would discipline the prisoner. He then gently picked up Adiya and helped her to her feet.

"Jenz, Greta's dad, then told the camp administrator that he would like to send some of the prisoners to work at the secret weapons plant in the north of Germany.

"We had already had our hair shaved off when camp administrator then told Jenz, "Pick out whoever you need, but be quick about it. Once they enter the tube to the gas chamber, I cannot save them."

"When there was some confusion on which people to save and send to the secret weapons center, Jenz took off his SS tunic and said to my dad, "Here, take my uniform jacket and cover the young woman you picked off the floor, then take the next five people in line.

"My older sister's eyes were briming with tears when she asked Greta's dad in a pleading voice, "May my younger sister come also?"

"And that, fellow students, ladies and gentlemen, is how my sister and I were 5 minutes away from the gas chamber and crematoriums at Treblinka in 1943.

A few people although stunned, began to clap. The clapping was sporadic but momentum grew. Within a minute, the entire auditorium was on its feet and clapping.

Chasha then stood and stretched out her arms with her palms out. "Thank you, from the bottom of my heart. But you should know, my friend Greta's story is much worse. I will hold the microphone close to her lips. It is difficult for her to talk, but she would like you to know her story.

Chapter 48

Greta's Incredible Story

"You wonderful people should know I was almost fifteen years when Jenz and Ezekiel first walked into a tiny restaurant my father owned in our small town in Nordhausen, Germany. Our country had very little to eat, but my father served the two officers in uniform some soup, crackers and dark bread. Nothing else was on the menu was available. My mother no longer could help at the restaurant. She had died from the typhus the year before.

"I apologized to both men for overhearing them making plans to get out of Germany before our country was defeated by the British, Americans, and Canadians from the west and the Russians from the east.

"I begged them to take me with them. Everyone in Germany knew the Red Army would destroy towns and villages and rape any young women they could capture. My dad encouraged me to ask if I could go with these two complete, but kind strangers in our army. I was firmly reminded that the Wehrmacht was no place for a pretty young teenager.

"About a year later these two men, now in civilian clothes returned to our small restaurant for a dinner meal. We were closed and couldn't afford to serve food anymore, but they were persistent in knocking on our door.

"We eventually let them in and gave them some leftover thin onion soup with some hard dark bread. During our meal, the Gestapo came to our door enquiring about two strangers who were observed entering our home.

"Although both of our guests were hiding in the kitchen, the Gestapo agents, after persistent questioning, became abusive and beat up and hurt my father. They then tied him to a chair and they both threatened to rape me in front of him if we didn't tell them where the two strangers were hiding. Both agents were armed and sinister.

The largest agent tore off my clothes, tied my hands behind me, and started raping me while holding a knife to my throat. I was screaming, my dad was crying. Jenz and Ezekiel then burst into the room. Ezekiel shot the tall agent who was hitting my father.

"Jenz pulled the other agent off me and placed him in a choke hold. I could hear the ugly agent's neck breaking. Both dead agents wound up in the trunk of Jenz and Ezekiel's automobile.

"About two weeks later my dad and I were listening to reports about the Russian advances into our country. That's when he decided to take me to the secret rocket base just outside of our town. He told me he loved me very much, but that he couldn't protect me from the Red Army.

"Needless to say, Jenz and Ezekiel were not at all pleased when I showed up. Both men indicated I could be shot for being on a secret army base without authorization. I asked them if my chances would be better with the Russian Army overrunning my village.

"I told the reluctant officers that I would change my gender and become their aide. After dying my hair black, darkening my complexion, wearing a tight tee-shirt to flatten my breasts, and cutting up a small army uniform, the two hesitant and cautious officers, my future dad, Jenz, and his best friend, Ezekiel, agreed that I probably would be safer with them than with the Red Army.

"We eventually came to America and lived in an old farmhouse on Concord Road. The house was owned by relatives of the Haynes Family and had been inherited by our family. No one had lived in the home since the 1920s; it was unheated with no plumbing, and rather basic wiring.

"This falling down farmhouse was like a palace for us. Our family consisted of my stepmom, Ilse, who had fallen in love with my stepdad, Jenz, while he was attending Hitler Youth Camp in 1936, and me. I must confess, my parents didn't adopt me – I adopted them! My name surprisingly appeared on our ship's manifest as their daughter when we sailed from Sweden to America.

"Our new life of living in Sudbury with dad working at Raytheon was shattered almost a month ago when I was taken from my classroom by Russian operatives. They kept me in the trunk of their automobile until they locked me in a cellar somewhere near Boston. The Russians wanted plans for something the Raytheon company was developing.

"While a prisoner in the cellar, I remembered a story my stepdad had told me about his being tortured by the Gestapo in Hamburg, Germany.

After he had killed the Gestapo Agent that was inflicting the torture, my dad opened a gas outlet in the basement of Gestapo Headquarters and left a couple of cigarettes burning on a chair. He then let the gas flood into the room and locked the door on the way out. The resulting explosion and fire leveled the building and destroyed all the evidence of his family's Jewish heritage.

"When I tried a similar feat in the locked cellar where I was held prisoner, I was able to escape through a small cellar window before the explosion and fire.

Unfortunately, one of the Russians agents captured me again, drugged me, and flew me to East Berlin, Germany. I was held in a secure Stasi prison, had most of my hair cut off, and thrust into an ice-cold shower.

"My dad and Ezekiel came to the prison in Russian Officer uniforms, but the warden sensed something was off and I was sent to a gulag over a thousand miles north of Moscow and almost one hundred miles above the Arctic Circle in Siberia.

"At the Vorkuta Gulag or prison, I was stripped of my Stasi Prison clothing, thrust into another cold shower, and shaved of all the hair on my head and private areas. When I resisted, I was slapped around and told I would be cut if I didn't cooperate.

"I was told that the guards would come around at night to seek sexual gratification from the female prisoners. The woman in the adjacent bunk warned me not to resist or that I would be severely beaten in addition to being raped.

"The next morning, I was raped again before being sent deep into one of the many coal mines at the gulag.

"Jenz and Ezekiel, dressed as Russian Army officers followed me at Vorkuta and searched for me in the coal mine. A planned explosion to loosen a coal seam also caused the collapse of the side tunnel where I was picking up coal to load into a coal trolly.

"Somehow, Jenz and Ezekiel found me in that collapsed tunnel trapped under a ceiling beam that had pinned me under some rocks and coal fragments.

"When we emerged from the mine, my dad and Zeke wanted to confront the guard who had been raping me. That guard found me in a crowd of other miners and grabbed me and pulled me into a small shed to, and I quote, "Continue the fun we had this morning!"

"My dad and Ezekiel had hidden themselves in the shed. The guard had hit me in the face so hard, he broke my nose, chipped some of my teeth, and blackened my eyes. My entire body was badly bruised when he threw me onto the wooden shed floor.

"As soon as the guard dropped his pants and started raping me, Jenz and Zeke jumped out of their hidden closets and pulled the monster off me. Zeke covered me with a towel and Jenz hit the giant ugly freak of a human being so hard on the back of his neck his vertebrae was crushed and he lost all control of his limbs.

"I want to apologize to the kind citizens of Sudbury for showing you what happened to me." As she was talking, Greta stood up from her chair; she unwrapped her scarf, removed her oversized sunglasses, and took off her floppy hat. A spotlight was switched on from the rear of the auditorium balcony.

"I know that the Russians were our allies during World War II. But, is this what friends to their allies?

There was an immediate gasp and murmur from the audience. Oh, my lord, someone blurted out. There wasn't a dry eye in the place. As Greta continued.

"I also want to apologize for my garbled speech this evening. I feel like I am trying to talk like a ventriloquist with my jaws wired together.

"Thank you for listening to Chasha and me and hearing about our journey to your wonderful town."

Both high school girls stood as thunderous applause, mixed with almost universal weeping, broke out.

Author's Notes

Readers should realize this novel is a continuation of the "Traitors" series of historical novels that describe many real situations and places. The protagonists are meant to give the reader a sense of fluency in the painfully onerous conditions in Germany and in the Nazi Concentration Camps during the Holocaust of World War II; and in the forced labor camps, the Gulags, in the Soviet Union, from the October Revolution in 1917 to the death of Stalin in 1953.

The fear and intimidation and the system of repression and punishment that the Gulag system of incarceration represented terrorized the entire Russian society. The threat of Nazi oppression and the concentration and death camps also threatened every citizen of Germany.

Mikhail Gorbachev came to power as the first president and last leader of the Soviet Union from 1985 to the country's dissolution in 1991. The Soviet Union broke apart because Gorbachev would not allow his military troops to stop, crush, and repress the revolution going on in the Eastern Bloc countries.

President Gorbachev was responsible for bringing **Glasnost** (transparency and openness) and **Perestroika** (restructuring) to the people of the Soviet Union and a diminution and virtual elimination of the fear and intimidation of the population from the slave labor camps or Gulags. Gorbachev wanted to reform the floundering Soviet economic system and compete with the United States, and be more competitive on the world economic stage.

He and then United States President Ronald Reagan were largely responsible for eliminating the Berlin Wall and ending the Cold War. In 1990, President Gorbachev was rewarded when he won the Nobel Peace Prize.

Words alone cannot possibly convey the climate of fear and intimidation that citizens of the Soviet Union endured during the time of Lenin and Stalin and perhaps even now under the current Putin administration.

This novel brings to the reader a glimpse of the cruelty and abhorrently difficult circumstances suffered by the completely innocent population of the Soviet Union.

The Gulag Archipelago by Aleksander Solzhenitsyn helped create the world we live in today – a world in which Soviet style communism is no longer held up as anybody's political ideal, and certainly no way to run a country! (From Anne Applebaum's introduction to this extraordinary book).

President Gorbachev briefly illuminated what Russia could become. A democratic Russia at peace with collaborative and rigorous competitive zeal would be a true blessing for its citizens and people everywhere.

J.H. Ahlin, Gloucester, Massachusetts. Summer 2024

Suggested Reading to help Understand the Gulag System of Prison Camps.

---

1. Solzhenitsyn, Aleksandr, *The Gulag Archipelago,* Three volumes, Harper & Row, New York, NY. 1976.

2. Applebaum, Anne, *Gulag, A History,* Anchor Books, A Division of Random House, Inc. New York, NY. May 2004.

3. Morris, Heather, *Cilka's Journey,* St. Martin's Publishing Group, New York, NY. 2019.
